Who Killed the Girls?

A Samantha Jones Murder
Mystery Thriller

AJ Newman

*

This book is dedicated to my beautiful wife of over thirty years.

Thanks go out to Carole Lewis and Michelle Butler who have been a big positive influence in my life and demonstrate doing the right thing every day. They were the ones that I bounced the plot off and gave me guidance.

Thanks to Christie Jenkins for proofreading and editing this novel.

✳

NOTE: My good friend Cliff Deane has four great Post-Apocalyptic novels on Amazon. If you like Post-Apocalyptic novels, you'll love these books.

Vigilante: Into the Darkness   Vigilante: Into the Fray

Vigilante: The Pale Horse   Vigilante: No Quarter

These books are available at Amazon:

https://www.amazon.com/dp/B06XG1XPQM

Please visit Cliff's Facebook page:

https://www.facebook.com/mustangpublishingllc

*

Books by AJ Newman

Alien Apocalypse:

The Virus   Surviving (Oct 2017)

A Family's Apocalypse Series:

Cities on Fire – Family Survival

After the Solar Flare - a Post-Apocalyptic series:

Alone in the Apocalypse   Adventures in the Apocalypse*

After the EMP series:

The Day America Died New Beginnings The Day America Died

Old Enemies The Day America Died Frozen Apocalypse

"The Adventures of John Harris" - a Post-Apocalyptic America series:

Surviving   Hell in the Homeland   Tyranny in the Homeland

Revenge in the Homeland...Apocalypse in the Homeland   John Returns

"A Samantha Jones Murder Mystery Thriller series:

Where the Girls Are Buried   Who Killed the Girls?

Books by AJ Newman and Cliff Deane

Terror in the USA: Virus: Strain of Islam

These books are available at Amazon:

http://www.amazon.com/-/e/B00HT84V6U

To contact the Author, please leave comments @:

Prologue

This novel is the second in a series of murder mystery novels starring Samantha Jones who is either blessed or cursed with the ability to encounter and solve crimes.

This series shows the development of a young abused girl into an amateur detective who solves crimes. She was abused, kidnapped and her new family attacked. She decided to fight back and find out "Where the Girls are Buried," in the first book and now danger lurks around every corner, but Sam won't be kept from solving, "Who Killed the Girls."

*

Chapter 1

Her mom slapped her and called her a prostitute when she came out of her bedroom dressed in short shorts and a halter-top.

"Get your butt back in your room and put something on that covers your belly. No daughter of mine leaves the house looking like a tramp."

She went to her room and put a T-shirt over the halter-top while her mom poured another vodka and orange juice. She was usually drunk every afternoon; she could barely walk and was slurring her words. Bridgette came out of her room and saw her mom passed out on the couch with the drink on her lap.

Bridgette rifled her mom's purse, took two hundred dollars and left the house saying, "Bye Mom. Drink yourself to death! I don't care anymore and won't be back. Oh, go look in the garage and you'll find Freddie. You'll need a new meal ticket. That perv won't hurt anyone else."

Her mom mumbled something and slumped down in the couch spilling her drink on the floor.

She went out beside the garage, retrieved her backpack and checked to make sure the knife was in the bag. She walked to Ms. Tapp's house to make a complete cut with life in Newton. She hated everything about Newton and its people except for her friend Kathy.

Ms. Tapp was just as bad as her stepdad and they both liked young girls. She had gone to the assistant principal to report the abuse from her stepdad and went from the frying pan into the fire. Ms. Tapp listened and allowed Bridgette to cry on her shoulder. She told Bridgette to give her a few days to get more evidence against him, but instead took Bridgette to her house and gave her some fruity drinks. Bridgette woke up early this morning naked and lying on a mattress in a basement. That is when she decided to handle things herself. She would make Freddie and Ms. Tapp pay for their sins and would then leave town. She watched CSI and knew that she could handle them, get away and start a new life.

She saw the house up ahead and decided to sneak in through the basement so she walked down the alley behind the houses until she was behind Ms. Tapp's house. She took the knife out of the backpack and hid the backpack in the bushes. She slowly walked in the shadows to the back of the house and broke a basement window with the knife handle. She unlatched the window and lowered herself into the basement. Just as she turned to head up the steps, a light came on and blinded her for a second. She refocused and saw Ms. Tapp had a big gun pointed at her.

"Well the little tramp came back to me. You should have left town and kept running. I'll make sure that the chain is tighter next time."

Grumpy was at the KSP headquarters for several hours being questioned about what he knew about Andy's death and Joe's disappearance. The two KSP officers who had met him at the hospital after the biker gang tried to kill him and his family was in the room and another guy in a suit who just listened. He told them about Jack Collins Jr. abusing his foster child, Sam, and her kidnapping. They all knew about the kidnapping of Grumpy's 15-year-old foster daughter, Sam, and that she shot Jack Collins Jr. to death defending Grumpy. Her dog Sammy saved them by attacking Jack and giving Grumpy enough time to hit Jack with a shovel. Sam had to shoot Jack to finish their escape and Jack died in the explosion at the cabin.

The senior officer asked, "Bill, I hear that you go by Grumpy. Do you want to be called by Bill or Grumpy?

"Bill will be fine. I'm just getting used to the Grumpy name. That's what people called me at work behind my back. I must have been a grouch back then."

"Ok Bill, tell us more about how Joe and Andy fit in to this."

"I think Andy and Joe were killed because they were investigating Jack Collins Jr. and that led them to something that Jack Collins Sr. did not want discovered."

The guy in the suit spoke up, "Do you know that Joe is dead? We have no proof that he is dead. Jack Collins Sr. is a pillar of the community, so be careful throwing his name around."

Grumpy got red in the face and said, "Are you on Collin's payroll? That sounded like a threat and not an unbiased statement."

"I'm sorry if it sounded that way. Collins has lawyers and contacts all over the state of Kentucky. He will sue anyone who says anything bad about him."

"Well you won't solve these two murders if you don't dig in his sandbox. Professionals have followed Andy, Joe and me. They looked like military types and Joe had to have his KSP buddies help him shake their tail car several times. I think they killed both Joe and Andy and are behind the gang who attacked my family."

"Do you know Nathan and Gail Cole?"

"Grumpy replied, "No, those names don't ring a bell. Wait a minute. Are they black and have a daughter named Kathy?"

The officer looked in a file and replied, "Yes they do. How do you know them?"

"I never met them, but Kathy Cole is my daughter Sam's best friend. Why do you ask about them?

"They were attacked and kidnapped earlier tonight. There was a lot of blood at the scene. Do you think this could be related to Jack Collins and the attacks on you and Sam?"

"Oh my God, this just is too much to be a coincidence. I'll be praying for their safety. Usually the simplest answer is the correct answer. Does Kathy know?"

"While she must have noticed that they did not come home on time, she doesn't know what happened. We picked her up a few minutes ago along with a CHFS caseworker. A janitor at the college saw the attack from half a mile away. He called it in, but by the time the campus police got there, the perp and the Coles were long gone."

"What are you going to do with Kathy?"

"Well, we normally turn children over to CHFS to take care of until we contact their families."

"My wife and I will be glad to keep her until her parents come back or family steps forward to care for her. Here is Greg Hope's home number. He is the Regional Director of CHFS for this area. He will okay it."

Grumpy gave him Greg's card and he called Greg and received approval for Grumpy to take Kathy home with him.

They escorted Grumpy to the waiting room where Kathy was talking with a woman. He walked in with the KSP officer and introduced himself to the CHFS caseworker.

"Hello, I am Bill Jones and I know Kathy."

Kathy saw Bill, ran to him and hugged him.

"Mr. Jones, mom and dad didn't come home and now the police came and got me and brought me here and I don't know what is going on. Where are my mom and dad?"

"Kathy, I just got here to take you home to stay with us until we figure this out. I don't know any more than you do. Come on with me and we will get you home and in bed. It's midnight."

The KSP officer told the caseworker that they had obtained approval from Greg Hope and she gave Grumpy a bag with Kathy's clothes and left the room.

One of the officers took Kathy and Grumpy to Grumpy's home since Grumpy's car was shot up during the biker gang attack earlier that day.

"Mary, wake up. There is a car pulling up into the driveway. It looks like a police car."

Mary woke up, grabbed her pistol and went to the window. She saw Grumpy getting out of the car and then saw Kathy with him.

She opened the door and said, "Hello Kathy come on in. What are you doing out so late."

Kathy started crying and said, "My mom and dad didn't come home."

Sam hugged Kathy and said, "You are welcome in our home anytime. Come on in and I'll get us some ice cream."

Mary said, "Boy that sounds good, I'll help."

They ate the ice cream and turned in for the night. Kathy, Sam and Sammy slept in Sam's room and talked for an hour before going to sleep. Sammy licked Kathy's face and sat in her lap until they went to bed for the night.

Sammy is Sam's Shih Tzu and is silver gray with dark eyes and a black button nose. His tail curls around and lies on his back when it's not shaking a mile a minute. He loves Sam and they are best friends. They both watch out for each other and give their life to save the other one. Sammy saved Sam's life several times during the kidnapping. He stopped one kidnapping attempt by Jack Collins Jr. by biting him and making him jump out of a second story window. Sammy, injured in the fall, quickly recovered.

"Ray, what the hell do you mean that things didn't go as planned? I paid you too much to allow things not to go as planned. What happened?"

"Sir, two of the targets were abducted and have disappeared. There was a failed attack on the family that resulted in a slaughter of the attackers and only minor injuries to the targets."

"Clean this mess up and deal with your team that failed."

"Mr. Collins, my team has disappeared. They did not come back for the other half of their money so I can only assume that they were eliminated."

"Ray, that makes no sense. The cops are missing and your guys are missing. One or the other should have showed up alive."

"Sir, I think that the two targets were eliminated, but when my senior contact tried to eliminate his team, things backfired on him."

"Is there any chance any of this crap will fall on my doorstep?"

"No sir. There is no connection to you at all."

Jack Collins Sr. exclaimed, "Dismissed!"

Jack Collins Sr. left the meeting thinking that Ray was wrong about there being no connections back to him. He made a call to sever that connection.

"Jerry, you said that if I ever needed your services to call you at this number."

"Jack, it's good to hear from you. I guess that I should be sorry that you have to call me, but even I have to make a living. Meet me at the lobby of the Radisson at 3:00. Don't worry about cash; I know that you are good for it."

Ray disappeared later that week.

Mary and Grumpy had been married over 25 years and lost two children. Mary was an attractive brunette woman in her late forties and was a stay at home mom and never worked outside of their home. Her son died in the war in the Middle East and her daughter committed suicide. They were devastated and had lost their way until they decided to become Sam's foster parents. Helping her helped heal their wounds. Sammy came with Sam and they were inseparable.

Mary woke up at 8:00, rubbed her eyes, rolled back over and fell asleep even with the pain from her wounds. She woke up an hour later, quietly dressed and went down stairs to start breakfast. She checked the security system and found no issues. All screens were clear so she made her usual pot of coffee and went out to the patio to enjoy the morning. A few minutes later Sam and Sammy joined her. Sam sat down beside Mary, laid her head on the table and pretended to be snoring.

"Baby we had a rough night. Are you okay?"

"Mom, besides being, kidnapped, chained in a cabin with a bomb, shooting Jack and shooting four biker thugs this has been a great month."

"You forgot the shotgun blast through my poor car's window and Bill and me getting shot. I wish I had killed that maniac when he hijacked us and kidnapped you."

Mary pointed at her shoulder sling.

Sam replied, "Yeah, that too."

She went into the kitchen and brought a cup and the pot out to refill Mary's cup.

"Mom, are y'all sorry that you became my foster parents? It has been freaking hectic since I joined the family."

"Sam, we can't wait to adopt you. Actually, we thought that you would be the devil's child from hell and we would barely survive the experience."

"Don't pat me on the back too soon. I know I'll screw up some more sometime."

"Don't worry, we all make mistakes. Families pull together when one of them make a mistake and help that one fix their mistake and move on."

Sam thought for a minute and a tear ran down her cheek.

She looked over at Mary, patted her own belly and said, "Is my baby a mistake?"

Mary went to her and took her in her arms and replied, "I can't lie to you and say it was planned, but most babies surprise their parents. Only a few plan everything out and say let's have a baby on December 5th. Babies come when they come. Your baby will have a Mom, two Grandparents and a fuzzy gray dog who all love it dearly."

"I love you Mom."

Kathy came down the stairs closely followed by Grumpy.

"Mary, Kathy and I are starving. How about some of your blueberry pancakes and bacon for breakfast?"

"Ok, I will teach the girls how to make pancakes while you call and check on Kathy's parents.

The girls had breakfast ready in about 30 minutes and Grumpy came back in the room and asked Mary to step outside with him.

"Mary, the Cole's kidnapping is all over the news and the police asked me to tell Kathy that her parents were kidnapped, but nothing else. They have contacted her grandparents and they are flying here from the west coast. They will be here late evening tomorrow. I volunteered to pick them up at the airport. I'll bring them here and we'll play it by ear from there."

"Let's tell her after breakfast. The poor child won't be hungry after this news."

They had a good breakfast and Sammy enjoyed getting a bite or two from everyone. He stayed close to Kathy and sat in her lap several times.

"Sam, please clean up the table and do the dishes while we pass on what we know to Kathy."

They took Kathy to the living room and Grumpy filled her in on what they knew so far. The news had most of the detail so Grumpy wanted to tell her before she saw it on the TV.

"Kathy, as you know your parents are missing. A janitor at the college your mom teaches at saw a man force them into his car and drive east. There was blood at the scene, but we don't know whose or if they're wounded. Kathy, that's all we know. All of this is on the news. Your Dad's parents are coming to be with you until we figure out what happened."

Kathy held her composure and said, "Mom and Dad are probably dead aren't they."

"Kathy, I won't speculate. It looks bad and the police have very little clues. There hasn't been a ransom note or any trace of them."

Kathy started crying and Mary held her and consoled her as best that she could. Sam joined them a little while later and took Kathy up to her room.

"Mary, something doesn't feel right here. I'd swear that this was connected to the attacks on our family, Joe and Andy, but I can't see any connection besides that Kathy is friends with Sam."

"Bill, we have enough to worry about. The attacks on us may just be starting. We both are recovering from gunshot wounds and I watch that darn security monitor every minute and wonder if someone is going to drive up shooting at the house. I might just start sleeping in the safe room."

Kathy Cole was Sam's only close friend in her high school. Sam's mom spent most of her money on drugs so Sam didn't have nice clothes and barely had any food. Kathy was several months older than Sam was, her parents were college educated and she was popular in school. She liked Sam because Sam didn't take any crap off anyone. Sam didn't look for trouble, but she didn't get out of its way either.

"Sam, do you think that whoever took my parents could be the same people behind the attacks on y'all? This is just too freaking weird. Two different families have people targeting them. It's just too much of a coincidence for me. I won't let myself cry and fret; I want to solve this and find the freaking bastards who took them."

"Kathy, I was thinking the same thing. I know that you hate Jack and his dad, but what did his dad ever do to you. Jack tried to corner you at my house, but did you ever meet his dad."

Kathy took a deep breath and said, "Jack's dad dropped by your house one day to give Jack something and I knocked on the door while he was in your house. He was drunk, pulled me into the house and tried to pull my shorts down. I kicked him on the shin and got away. He yelled that he would kill me as I ran away."

"We need to keep our investigation of Mr. Jack Collins going and find the dirt on him. I hate to say it, but I may have to ask Jeff to help us."

"Sam, you know he knows the internet and computers better than most adults. He really likes you."

"I'll call him after lunch."

*

Chapter 2

Sam and Kathy set the table as usual and when they all sat, Sam said, "Is it ok if I give grace?"

Grumpy looked at her and said, "Of course."

Sam bowed her head and prayed, "God please watch over Kathy's family and my new mom and dad. Please bring Kathy's parents back to her safely. Bless this food and thank you for the blessing that we receive every day."

Sam looked up and Grumpy said, "Very good. I am so proud of you."

Sam and Grumpy still wanted to find out if Jack's father, Jack Collins Sr., had been involved with the dead girls and were conducting their own investigation. This made

Collins Sr. very mad and he was trying to get them to stop before they ruined his run for the governor's job.

"Hello, Jeff? Sam wants to speak with you."

Jeff lived a short distance down the road from Grumpy's house. He was 17, tall and had bright red hair. He was a computer nerd who liked sports and Sam.

Kathy cupped her hand over the phone and handed it to Sam. Sam made ugly faces at her and took the phone.

"Hey Jeff"

"Hello Sam, are you okay? I saw the news about that gang attacking you. Do you think it's related to the other issues?"

"Thanks for asking. We are all okay, but yes, I think it's the same people. Jeff we need some internet help. Can you please come over and help us?

"Sam, I'm worried about you. I'm busy this weekend. My aunt and my cousins are visiting; can it wait until Monday after school?

"Yes, why don't you ride home with dad and me?

"Okay."

"Thanks."

Sam punched Kathy on the arm and said, "You pig; now he'll think I like him."

"Well you do."

"Do not. We need to get to work. Pull up the maps that mark the hometowns of the missing girls. I'll pull up the police reports for the ones we haven't looked at yet."

"Sam this is exciting and could be fun if these girls weren't dead. I want to solve crimes for living people."

"Kathy, many of these murders are cold cases and no one is trying to find out who kidnapped these girls. I pray each night that they are alive. Then I think about what they could be going through and death doesn't seem so bad."

"Did Sam Smith just say that she prayed? You gave grace at lunch."

"What's the big deal?"

"Samantha Smith, I tried to get you to go to church with me and you just laughed and said that you didn't believe in God."

"Well Mary and Grumpy believe in him and I like them so it must be rubbing off on me. They don't push me and I like that, but the more I am around them I feel better thinking that there is a God watching over us."

"I was raised going to church and have always believed in god, but I am mad because he didn't stop the kidnapping."

"I have trouble with that also, but our pastor says that God doesn't step in and save us every day. God influences us to do good and help ourselves. Perhaps he will influence us to kick the asses of the people that have kidnapped your parents."

"You are so bad. You go from inspiring to kicking ass all in the same discussion."

"Well I took serious that part of the bible that says, "God helps those who help themselves and what about the one that says, *An eye for an eye?*"

"Let's change the subject. When will you go out on a date with Jeff? He really likes you."

"Duh, remember that I am the pregnant girl who's getting fatter by the day. I can't go 10 minutes without having to pee and I eat like a horse. Great date that would be! No boy wants to date a knocked up fat girl as big as a barn, especially one that is having a baby with a serial killer as its father."

"Sam, you are beautiful and will be skinny after the baby is born. I wish I was skinny and had boobs like yours. Do you hope that you keep them after the birth?"

"I don't care."

"Girl, the boys love big boobs!"

"Kathy I don't have time for boys. Let's get to work."

"Yes Master, don't beat these tired old bones."

The next morning after church, Mary knocked on Sam's door, joined them and asked, "What are you two up to this morning?"

"Oh nothing, just talking"

"Sam, I found some of the print outs on the missing girls. Be careful and don't draw attention to us. Collins is a dangerous and violent man. Bill and I want to help, but above all, we can't let anyone know that you are investigating Collins."

"Mom, we aren't investigating Collins. We are looking into the missing girls from the area."

Mary laughed and said, "Don't BS me girl. We both know down deep inside that, he is involved in some way. Bill and I want to sit down with you two and give you some ground rules that should keep us all safe. Bill might even pull in that security consultant again to show us how to do this covertly."

"Mom that would be great! We'll show you what we have when y'all are ready."

"Mrs. Jones, do you think that he killed my mom and dad?"

"Now child, we don't know that they are dead. They are missing and yes, I feel that he is involved."

Mary left and they played with Sammy for a few minutes and got back to work. Sammy tried to keep them rough housing with him, but the poor little Shih Tzu was out of luck, so he went down stairs and barked at the back door until Mary let him out. He headed straight to the garage to see if Grumpy would play with him. Mary followed to check on Grumpy before lunch. He was rubbing Sammy's ears when Mary walked up.

"Bill, could you put a doggie door in the back door so Sammy can come and go without making me be a doggie butler? I love him, but he can be a pest when I'm busy."

"Yes Dear."

"Yes Dear, what? Are you going to install the door?"

"Now Mary, when did you ever not get me to do what you wanted me to do?"

Sammy barked and ran to Mary.

"See Sammy agrees. Hey, what are the girls up to this morning and how is Kathy taking the bad news?"

"On the surface she is handling it better than a teen should, but I think it just hasn't sunk in yet. She'll be bawling her eyes out in a day or so. I hope her grandparents stay with us for a while so Sam can help her through this crisis."

"Mary, would you have believed a few months back that you would count on Sam to help another girl through a crisis? She was a wreck when we became her foster parents."

"You are right. I hoped for the best and expected the worst. Bill we need to start the adoption process. She needs to be reassured that she and her baby are wanted and loved."

"Mary, I agree. Please call Greg at CFHS and see how we proceed."

She gave Grumpy a big kiss and went back to the house. Sammy jumped in Grumpy's arms and tried to lick his face.

"So Sammy, you want to be adopted also. We can do that too. You are now Sammy Jones instead of Sammy Smith. Darn, I never thought that. We are the Jones and we are adopting a girl with Smith as her last name. Jones and Smith sound like made up names."

Grumpy continued working on his old F1 Ford truck until lunch and then washed up and went to the house. Of course, he had to stop and play fetch with Sammy several times on the way. Since Sam and Sammy had entered his life, Grumpy had become a different person. He got the name Grumpy for always arguing politics and being a bit gruff at work. Mary still called him Bill, but sometimes slipped and said Grumpy. The deaths of their two children, Ann and Johnny, made him even grumpier.

He walked into the kitchen and saw the girls setting the table and Mary was getting ready to serve lunch.

"What's for lunch? Sammy and I are hungry."

"Poor starving things. I didn't fix any lunch for you two since you ate so much for breakfast."

"That's not funny. Sammy, bite the mean old woman."

25

Sammy just sat there beside Sam and looked at Grumpy like he was crazy."

"Old? That dog knows who feeds and cares for him. Right Sammy? And besides, that old comment had better not be said again."

Sammy ran to Mary, licked her leg and wanted Mary to pick him up. Kathy picked him up and said, "She is cooking and we don't want Sammy hair all over our food."

"Girls, we're going to pick up Kathy's grandparents at the airport at 4:00 and I'm going into town after supper to rent a van until the car gets out of the shop. You all need to be ready to leave at 2:00 so we can get the van and go to the Louisville airport. Kathy can you tell us anything about your grandparents?"

Mr. Jones, they are in their late fifties and Nana, Martha, has always been a stay at home housewife and Gramps, GW, was in the Air Force and then a police officer until he retired. He was a homicide detective for the last 15 years before he retired at 52 after being shot several times. They aren't rich, but are doing ok. They planned to move here next year after Gramps finished fixing up their house to sell. Nana is a lot like Mrs. Jones she likes cooking, reading and gardening. Gramps hunts, fishes and flies remote controlled airplanes. You will like them."

"What does the GW stand for in your Gramp's name?"

"George Washington. He was named after George Washington Carver."

"So, George and Martha must get a little kidding about their names."

"That's why Gramps goes by GW to avoid the kidding and jokes."

They picked up the van, drove to Louisville International Airport and arrived early so they watched the planes taking off and landing before heading to meet the Coles. They only had to wait for 15 minutes before they spotted the Coles passing past the security checkpoint and Kathy ran to greet them. She was hugging a very attractive black woman who looked much younger than early fifties, but Grumpy didn't see her Gramps. Then a tall man walked up with two roller bags in tow and Kathy jumped in his arms and almost knocked him down. She started crying and it took several minutes for the three of them to regain their composure.

"Mary, Bill and Sam, these are my grandparents, GW and Martha."

They shook hands, and then Grumpy invited them to supper and stay at his home during their visit.

"Bill, we hate to impose on you. We can stay at the Westbrook which I believe is five miles from your place."

"GW, we'd love to have you at our home. We have plenty of room and perhaps we can help you during your visit."

"Gramps please stay with the Jones. Please?"

"Ok, I was actually hoping that you would offer. Sam and Kathy are so close and I think she needs her friend right now. Also, I know you are wondering how a white guy married to a black woman got a name like George Washington Carver Cole."

Grumpy replied, "Hadn't grossed my mind," and broke out laughing.

"Well my dad and mom were in school at Ohio State and had a white racist professor and when I came along they named me after Mr. Carver to piss him off. Then I met Martha on the first day in an American History class at UK and the professor was performing roll call. He was black and when he called my name, a big smile came over his face until he saw me. Right in front of the class, he put me down for being white with a great black man's name. Martha and the others were laughing at him and told him that it would have honored Mr. Carver for anyone to name their baby after him. Martha and I started dating and swore that our children would be named normal names."

Mary spoke up, "That is a darling story. You are a beautiful couple and I'm glad that Kathy brought us together. Bill is grilling some steaks and corn on the cob; I'm fixing the baked potatoes and chocolate pie. Let me know if you have any special diet restrictions or don't like what I'm cooking and I'll fix what you like.

Martha answered, "If it was once alive, GW will eat it. He likes his steaks thrown on the grill, seared on both sides and bloody in the middle. I like mine medium. All of the food sounds wonderful and we like home cooking and aren't fancy people."

"Great, that describes us also."

Grumpy said, "All this talking about food is making me hungry."

"Me too"

After shown to their rooms, they had an excellent supper. Afterwards, Martha took Kathy into their room to reassure her and try to make her feel safe. GW and Grumpy walked out to the garage so Grumpy could show GW his trucks. Sammy followed and ran ahead of them.

"Bill before we look at the trucks can you fill me in on what you know about my son and his wife's disappearance? I called a friend in the KSP and he said that there have been several unsolved murders in this area and he told me about the attacks on your family and Sam's kidnapping. I also noticed that you have a gun under your shirt. Should we be worried about Kathy and our safety?"

"GW, first I wish I could answer that y'all are safe here with us. I can't say one way or another on that. I think that you'd be safer taking your wife and Kathy back to the west coast and forgetting about investigating your son's disappearance. I do believe that the attacks on us, the disappearance of your family and the murders of over fifty young girls are all connected."

"I'm a homicide cop and I believe my son has been murdered and I am going to stay and dig into the investigation. I brought my Glock and I know how to protect myself. Who is this Collins guy? The internet has the facts about his business, wealth and politics, but who is he and how did he get so rich so quick? Did he kill my son?"

"GW, everyone who has investigated Collins over the years was bought off, scared off or had an unfortunate accident. The SOB is a very powerful man who meets with the president and is setting the stage to run for Governor of Kentucky. Any issues stirred right now will be frowned upon and dangerous. This guy has deep pockets and hires professionals to do his bidding. He went on to fill him in on all of the details."

GW was holding Sammy while rubbing his ears and responded, "Where do my son and daughter in law fit in to this mystery?"

"I'm not sure, but I think Kathy and Sam were investigating Collins and the missing girls through the internet and were detected. I had warned Sam to only search through our home system because we have a fancy protection system that makes us impossible to trace. Kathy used your son's laptop to search Collins industries in an attempt to break through all of the shell companies and track where he gets money from and whom he donates it. The couple disappeared within a couple of days after Kathy searched his information."

"So Kathy doesn't know that her search may have led Collins to my son?"

"No, I don't want her thinking that she has any responsibility for her parent's deaths."

"Thanks, that's what I would have done myself. As much as it pains me to say it, I know that Nathan and Gail are dead. There was no request for ransom and a lot of blood at the crime scene. Tell me more about your internet security."

"GW, it's not just internet security. I had a consultant install a complete security system and a safe room so I could be prepared to do battle with Collins. Let's start behind the garage."

Grumpy showed him the shooting range, motion detectors and CCTV cameras on the outside then took him in the house to see the monitors, the safe room and their weapons.

GW was examining one of Grumpy's AR-15s and said, "Wow, I feel safer now, but what about your security away from home. Your family was attacked and Sam kidnapped away from home. You have spent a small fortune to increase your homes safety, but do you have the cash to improve your safety away from home?"

"We're not rich, but thanks to an inheritance we have some extra dollars. What do you suggest?"

"I will think about it, but I think you probably need to have your consultant back to give you some recommendations. Short of a bullet proof car and armed escorts, there is nothing that gives a 100 percent guarantee that a bad guy can't shoot you from a hundred yards away."

"That's what I've been thinking and frankly has slowed me down on continuing the investigation. I've kept the girls limited to internet searches, but those two think they are Sherlock Homes and Mr. Watson. What are your plans? Are you taking Kathy back to the west coast?"

"No, I plan to stay here with Kathy while I poke around and catch the bastards who killed Nathan. I could use some help."

"Yes, we need to join forces and stop this madman before more innocent people get hurt. Why don't y'all stay with us until you sell your home and move here? We have plenty of room and I think it would be good for Kathy and Sam."

"I don't want to impose, but it makes sense if we are going to work closely on this case. Don't you need to check with Mary?"

"She suggested it this morning when she heard that you were a retired homicide investigator. She knew that you couldn't sit on the sidelines and watch this get swept under the rug like the rest."

"Once a cop always a cop. Why do you trust me? You have shown all of your security to a total stranger."

"I'm a pretty good judge of character and Sammy is sitting in your lap trying to lick your face. If Sammy likes you then I trust you. That dog is more than just a dog. I know that sounds a bit wacky, but sometimes I think he is a cross between Sam's guardian angel and a pit bull dog. He saved Sam and me several times and put his life on the line each time."

"Good dog."

Sammy stood up in GW's lap and looked him in the eye and then jumped into Grumpy's lap and lay down while they talked about the trucks.

*

Chapter 3

Kathy stayed home with her grandparents and missed her parents with all of her heart. GW borrowed the van and took her to her house so she could get some clothes and check on the house.

"Kathy we plan to stay with the Jones for a while, but what do you think about us living in your house at least until your mom and dad return?"

"Gramps, I'm only 16, but I know that my mom and dad were killed by that Collins scumbag. He didn't do it himself; he only abuses young girls. He hasn't got the guts to try to hurt an adult."

"Dear, did he hurt you?"

"No Gramps, but he tried. I kicked him and run like hell back home, but I know what he wanted. The bastard is a pedophile and I think he sells some of the girls he has kidnapped."

"I thought that was his son doing the kidnapping and killing the girls."

"Yes, but the police said some of the bodies date back to when Jack Jr. was a small boy and they are buried at Jack Senior's cabin that has been in the family since the late 1800's. I'll bet they are still finding bodies."

"I'll ask around and see what the police have to say."

"The police are afraid of Collins. Some work for him and the rest are scared of him. That's why Sam and I are going to get the dirt on him and put his ass under the jail."

Martha spoke up, "Kathy those are rough words for a young lady. Please don't lower yourself to use that kind of language."

"Yes Mam."

GW snooped around the house looking in all of the nooks and crannies. He searched the basement, garage and attic and found nothing suspicious. He examined the office and reviewed every bill, letter and document in the room, which took several hours and found nothing. His son and Gail had a large 401k savings, paid their bills on time, had a large insurance policy on both of them and the house was paid for. His car, was still held for evidence, but Gail's Jaguar was in the garage along with several bicycles and kayaks. As he went back in the house, he noticed the key pad for the alarm system and thought about security. He looked around the room, looked under the desks and performed a sweep of the room for bugs.

He found one in the office and others in the master bedroom and living room. He left them all in place.

"Dear, let's take Kathy to get a burger; I'm hungry. I'll drive the Jag and you two take the van."

They entered the restaurant, the waiter seated them and they ordered their lunch. They talked about how nice the Jones family was and enjoyed their lunch.

"Don't be alarmed, but the house is bugged with listening devices and may have cameras. I didn't see any cameras, but I don't put it past these bastards."

Martha frowned.

"I'll have a professional use electronics to sweep the house and then we will start sending a message to these assholes."

"GW!"

"Martha, I am not a child and Kathy is a young woman. Detectives talk rough."

"Well you might talk that way, but Kathy had better not in my presence."

"Yes, Ma'am"

"Okay, let's eat and I want to check in with Grumpy to see if he has found any bugs at his place."

"I thought his name was Bill."

"It is. His friends and people that don't like him call him Grumpy. I like Grumpy."

All of Sam's teachers and her classmates had seen the story on TV about the motorcycle gang's attack on Sam and he foster parents. Each teacher asked Sam to tell the class a short version of the event and then tried to focus them on their schoolwork. Sam was a hero again. Everyone tried to be around her all day. At lunch, she saw Jeff sitting off by himself reading a book while he munched on a sandwich.

"Jeff, can I sit with you?

"Yes, I'd like that. I was worried about you. Are your mom and dad ok?

"Yes, they are okay. They shot up the car and we all got a few scratches, but most of the gang is dead. Why are you worried about me?

"Sam, I like you and would like to see more of you. I want to hang out with you if you'd like to."

"Jeff, I've never dated or anything and I feel backwards around boys. I do like you and I will hang out with you, but you have noticed that I am growing bigger and bigger every day. I'm not going to get in the back seat of your car and make out either."

Jeff started laughing and said, "Sorry, but you are so pretty when you try to be mean and sarcastic. I really like you and I won't hurt you. When is the baby due?"

"I'm about 5 months along. You don't mind that I'm having another guy's baby?"

"Sam, I don't want to hurt you, but I'd guess that the father is dead. I have always liked you, but I was always too scared to talk with you. I came by your house a couple of times and Jack pulled a gun out and ran me off. I'm more comfortable with computers and math then women. You have always been hot to me and I want to be around you. I'll help you with your detective stuff, but please don't get me shot."

She turned red and started to say something.

"I'm just kidding, chill."

"You think I'm hot?"

She looked at him and saw that he was staring in her eyes. Looking into his eyes, she became flush and choked up. His face was almost as red as his hair.

Jeff changed the subject, "Hey, I just heard that Kathy's friend Bridgette moved out of town. Her mom killed her stepdad and committed suicide. Her grandparents came and took her to Idaho. She stabbed him twenty times. It will be on the news today."

"Darn, that was Kathy's only other friend. I didn't like her because she was always trying to act tough. She was always smoking and showing off her big boobs. You boys need to keep your minds on other things besides boobs."

"I'm keeping my mouth shut because you'll either hit me or think I'm gay if I try to answer that one."

"Smart boy. Now stop thinking about boobs and tell me how you can help us get the dirt on Collins."

"You brought up boobs, I didn't. Forget it, I plan to hack into Jack Junior's and Senior's e-mail and see what's there first. Then we'll keep peeling back the onion on his businesses."

"What can Kathy and I do while you check e-mails?"

"I need help searching the e-mails and any data that I find. This will take many hours of reading and cross referencing his information."

"I know that you are smart and all with computers, but how did you learn how to perform the detective work with the internet and data stuff."

"I watch several crime shows on TV and I searched the internet and bought some books on how to be a detective."

"Can I read them? Please?"

"Yes, we need to get good at this or we'll get caught and everyone who has crossed Collins runs into bad luck."

"Jeff, you can do your internet searches from our house. Dad had a security guy fix it so we can't be traced on the internet."

"I want to see that. Meet you out front after school."

They drove back to Grumpy's house after lunch and GW found him in the garage working on the old truck.

"Grumpy, are you sure that your security is actually secure here at the house and garage?"

"Yes, and I have the house and garage swept for devices once a week. We have the cameras, listening devices and motion detectors guarding the place. We only talk about sensitive subjects in the house or garage to reduce someone trying to eavesdrop. What is your concern?"

"I found three bugs at my son's house. These aren't cheap do it yourself stuff, but expensive professional grade. This has to relate to Collins and Sam somehow. The only connection is Kathy."

Do you want the security group I use to sweep the place?

"No, after thinking about the bugs, I wonder what they expected to hear and then what information that we want them to hear."

"A disinformation campaign"

"Ye, but I'm not sure what I want them to hear."

"GW, we don't have to know what we need them to hear right now. You might mention a few things like someone at Nathan's work had threatened him to throw him off course. We just don't know enough now. Let's go into my war room and I'll fill you in on what we know and then we need to narrow our goal down."

Grumpy took him to the back of the garage and into the office. There were maps on the wall, whiteboards covered in writing and a wall covered in sticky notes and a few photos of people.

"You have a lot of information on these walls. I see info on Collin's business, his acquaintances and many dead or missing people. What I don't see are any connections to Collins."

"GW, I would guess that Collins has someone doing his dirty work. We need to find out who that is and we might be able to pin something on Collins."

"Collins Industries is a large multinational company and it will have a large security group. I'll snoop around, get a list of who works in security for Collins and get background checks. Now what about our goals?"

"We started out just trying to protect Sam from Jack Jr. and were dragged into looking at Jack Sr. That's when the serious attacks started. What is your goal? I can stop now and I think that my family will be safe. I just have to make Collins think that we are leaving him alone."

"My goal is to find the bastards who killed my son and daughter in law and put them behind bars. I don't even know Collins and could care less about him, but if he is involved, I'm taking him down."

Grumpy went to the whiteboard and wrote, "*Find Killers.*"

"My goal is to find who attacked us and eliminate the threat."

Grumpy wrote that on the board and said, "I agree on Collins. While I am confident that our goals are the same, let's stay unbiased and see where our investigations take us."

"I agree. I'll check in with my friend in the Louisville PD and I guess you can check in with the KSP."

"Again, I agree. We do need to discuss the girl's playing detective. I'm thinking Nathan was killed because Collin's security discovered his PC was being used to investigate Collins. How do we handle the girls?"

"I think that we sit down with them and get them to tell us what they are doing and determine the risk. If they can help by safely feeding us data from the internet then ok, but if they are doing anything that can be tied back to us, then we have to shut them down."

"I was thinking the same thing. Let's go see what the wives are doing and then I have to go pick Sam and Jeff up at school.'

"Who is Jeff?"

"He is a friend of Kathy and Sam's and wants Sam to be his girlfriend. I hear that he is a genius with PCs and the internet."

"Grumpy, please don't take this wrong, but what boy wants to date a pregnant girl? Most would be avoiding her."

"Apparently he has had a crush on her for a while and sees the bigger picture, but I agree with you. I would have walked across the street to avoid being seen with a pregnant girl when I was their age."

Grumpy only had to wait a few minutes before he saw Sam standing by the front door of the school. There were a couple of girls talking with her when he saw Jeff walk out of the front door and join them. He pointed at Grumpy and they walked towards the truck talking and laughing.

"Hello Mr. Jones, how are you today?"

"I'm doing ok. How are you and your folks?"

"We're all doing okay. Mom and Dad are out of town at one of his conventions, so I am by myself for a couple of days."

They drove away from the school and Jeff said, "I really like your truck. I want one like it when I get enough money saved up."

"Do you have your license?"

"Yes, I'm 17."

"Do you want to drive us home?"

"Yes, are you sure?"

"Yes, it's back roads and not much traffic. Just drive carefully. You do know how to drive a stick shift, don't you?"

"Yes sir, my Grampa lets me drive his truck and the farm truck all over his farm. He has one that looks like this, but it is rusty and barely runs. I plan to make it into a custom pick up one day."

Grumpy changed seats with the boy and claimed the passenger window side so Sam was sitting next to Jeff. They only had about five miles to the house, but Jeff enjoyed driving the truck and had many questions about it. Grumpy told him where to park and they went into the house.

"Honey we're home."

"Hello Jeff, good to see you again. I have a great supper prepared. Sam, Kathy is upstairs. Y'all go ahead and join her."

"Hey Jeff"

"Hey Kathy, I'm sorry about your parents. Sam filled me in on the information that wasn't on the news. Are you okay?"

"I'm not okay, but I am mad and want to kick someone's butt."

"Like I said, Sam filled me in, but what can we do to help you. Our search was to get the dirt on Collins, but I guess that you want to find the people who kidnapped your mom and dad."

Kathy replied, "I think all of this is tied together. I just don't think that several murders, kidnappings and attacks are all a coincidence. This is a small town and this stuff only happens once every two or three years."

"Kathy, have you heard about your friend Bridgette?"

"Is she dead?"

"No, her mom killed her stepdad and then killed herself. Bridgette's grandparents took her to Idaho.

Sammy started barking and running around in circles on the bed; jumping on everyone.

"I agree with Sammy that sounds like BS to me. Why would they come get her and leave before a funeral?"

"Sam, you are right and again two more murders and maybe a kidnapping? Bridgette would have called me. She was a messed up girl, but a good friend."

"Kathy was she ever around either of the Collins? This is weird."

"No, but she told me that someone at the school had... "

She stumbled and looked at Jeff and said, "I'm kind of embarrassed to say this with Jeff in the room. She said that a teacher at school was getting her drunk and having sex with her."

"Was it Mr. Lee? I always knew that he was a perv."

"No she said that it was a woman."

"Yuck, gross, "said Jeff.

"That's too much information. So now we're solving sex crimes."

"Dummy, what do you think Jack and his dad were doing to those young girls that were killed?"

"I'm not stupid, but I guess that it just got real when we talked about it just now. It makes me sick that anyone would hurt a young girl."

He was sitting beside Sam on the bed and found himself holding her hand. They looked at each other and then Sam stood up and walked across the room to her desk.

43

"Kathy, keep looking up missing girls, I'll map what you find and Jeff I think that you should keep after Collins' business."

"Sam, before I start on Collins, I'm going to check on Bridgette. Her grandparents shouldn't be hard to find and we'll call her."

"Great idea!"

They got busy with their parts of the investigation and a half hour later Jeff asked for them to look at his laptop.

"Jeff, what is that? It looks like Bridgette's school records. How did you pull them up?"

"Don't worry about how. A good hacker can get anyone's records. Look at this!"

He pointed at the bottom of the second page. They saw that her grandparents on her mom's side were deceased and her dad's father had died several years back. Her Grandmother lived in Maine. There was a contact number and Jeff dialed the number into his iPhone and placed it on speaker."

They heard, "Morning Gale Nursing Home, how may I help you?"

Jeff replied, "Can I speak to Mrs. Robinson?"

"Sir, Mrs. Robinson had a stroke three years ago and hasn't spoken a word since then."

"I'm sorry, but is this Hellen Robinson?"

"Yes."

"Is her granddaughter with her? Bridgette Payne?"

"No, who is this?"

"I'm a friend of her granddaughter and I can't find her."

"Just a minute, there it is. I have her mother's number."

"Mam, her mother is dead."

Jeff hung the phone up and stared at the other two and said, "This is not good news. If Bridgette isn't with her grandma, then where the hell is she?"

"Now Kathy, don't assume that she is dead. There may be something that we are missing."

"Sam, we need to find out who is the perv messing with my friend and we will find Bridgette."

Just then, Mary called them to supper.

"We thank you Lord for this food and watching over us and keeping us all safe. Amen."

Grumpy was getting better at saying grace and never be accused of being long winded.

Mary had prepared a roast with carrots, new potatoes and corn. She also had pecan and chocolate pies in the oven. The food was delicious and GW and Jeff asked for second helpings. Sam ate very slow, but soon asked for a second helping.

Grumpy said, "Well how was school today?"

Sam replied first, "Just the usual. I had a history test and everyone wants to know what I'm going the name the baby. Just regular high school stuff."

Kathy added, "My friend Bridgette had a tragedy in her family. Her mom killed her stepdad and then killed herself. Our Vice Principal told everyone that Bridgette's grandparents drove down from Idaho and took her back home with them."

Mary said, "That's terrible and I'm so sorry for your friend's loss. It seems strange that they would leave before the funeral."

Jeff spoke up and said, "What's really strange is that we found that she only has one grandmother and she is in a rest home in Maine. She had a stroke and can't speak, much less drive down here form Idaho or Maine."

"Whoa! So where is Bridgette?"

"We don't know, but we do know that a teacher at the school was abusing her after school at her house."

GW said, "Wait a minute. That's a lot of info you are bombarding us with. Slow down for a minute. How do we know about the abuse?"

Kathy replied, "Gramps, about two months ago Bridgette told me that her stepfather was trying to force her to have sex with him when her mom was gone. She went to Ms. Tapp and told her about her stepdad and Ms. Tapp told her that she would handle it with the authorities. Well, Bridgette told me nothing changed at home and then last week she told me that someone from school was getting her drunk and abusing her. That's all I know."

"How well do y'all know this Ms. Tapp?"

Sam answered, "Everyone knows her at school. She is the assistant principal. I have talked with her a dozen times and she never hit on me. She just tried to get me to do better in my classes."

Kathy said, "Same here."

Jeff replied, "Never talked with her."

"Grumpy, for a small sleepy town, y'all sure have a lot of murders and another missing young girl."

"It just dawned on me that we need a profile for each of the missing girls to see what attracts the kidnappers in the first place. That will help us with motivation and help predict more kidnappings."

"Sam, that's a great idea! Can you and Kathy add that to your current information on the missing girls? Don't look surprised. Grumpy filled me in on the work that you are doing. We need to keep you safe, but I would like you to keep up the investigation as long as it's done with the safety of the internet security at this house. Okay girls and you too Jeff."

They all agreed to do all searches from the security of the Jones home.

They went back upstairs to Sam's room and started searching the internet and reviewing e-mails.

Kathy got their attention and said, "Sam, Mr. Jones has been teaching you how to shoot guns, hasn't he? I want to learn also. Do you think he would mind if Gramps teaches me on your shooting range?"

"Kathy, this may not be the best time with having just lost your parents. You might shoot the wrong people."

"I just want to learn to protect myself. Jeff don't you want to learn how to shoot and defend yourself?"

"I have been shooting and hunting since I was 10 years old. I have a 12 Gauge shotgun, a .308 deer rifle and a .22 automatic pistol. I know how to shoot, but I want to use my mind to keep myself out of trouble not a gun. I love guns, but once that bullet leaves the gun you can't bring it back."

Sam knew her friend wouldn't change her mind so she said, "Then ask your Gramps and if he agrees, then he can ask Dad."

*

Chapter 4

The room was cool and smelled like crap. Her mouth was dry and she tried to lap the water from the bowl to quench her thirst, but couldn't reach the water. She forced her head into the bowl and could just touch the water with the tip of her tongue. She was naked, blindfolded and her hands tied behind her back. There was a chain wrapped around her right ankle just tight enough not to come off. It was just long enough to allow her to move in a ten-foot circle around a steel pole. There was a five-gallon bucket for a toilet and bread and water on the table. Ms. Tapp emptied the bucket before she went to school each morning. The water bowl would be filled and bread thrown on the table at the same time. The bucket was in a corner of the small room and was across from the table. She had to eat and drink like a dog. She tried to remove the blindfold by rubbing it on the edge of the table, but finally realized tape kept it on her face.

At night, she lay on a mattress and a blanket thrown over her. She thought that she must be in a basement because it was very quiet and smelled musty like basements tended to do. She was afraid to sleep though sleep always won. She would wake up trying to scream, but no one could hear her muffled voice.

She had never prayed before in her life, but when the bitch brought the man down to the basement, she started that night. She fought the first couple of times and received a burning pain in her side each time. One shock made her pass out. She woke with him on top of her. She knew it had to be a stun gun and couldn't bear the pain so she stopped resisting. She tried not thinking about what was happening so she tried several things to keep her mind off the degradation. She sang songs in her head, thought of numerous ways to kill Ms. Tapp and him before praying. She didn't know how to pray so she just said what was on her mind.

She asked the Lord, *"Why is this happening to me. I know I'm bad, but this is so mean and cruel."*

The abuse continued for several days and her prayers changed to, *"Please stop this. Please. Please."*

She gave up and went back to thinking of ways to kill them both. This kept her going through the pain and abuse. She just knew that she would live through this ordeal, find them and make them pay for what they have done to her.

One evening Ms. Tapp game down the steps and said, "We have to make you pretty so one of our clients will want you. There is soap and water on the table."

50

Ms. Tapp removed the blindfold and she saw that a man was standing there with a mask over his face. He had a video camera.

Bridgette, I'm going to remove your handcuffs and help you clean yourself up and dress you in these pretty clothes and makeup. If you resist, he will shock you until you do what we want so don't make it any harder on yourself. If you don't resist, you will have pizza for supper."

"Why do you want to dress me up and take pictures for your clients?"

"Don't worry about that just wash up and get dressed."

"Are you selling me to some dirty old man like this creep?"

The man walked over to her, stuck the stun gun to her side, gave her a quick shock and said, "Shut up and get dressed."

She started washing her face and then put the clothes on. The dress looked like something an eight year old would wear and the bitch put her hair in pigtails.

She thought, *"I have to play along and keep them happy to live long enough to come back here and kill both of them."*

She burned his detail into her mind. There was a tattoo of a coiled snake on his left forearm and a knife on his right arm. He had a three-inch scar long behind his ear that wrapped around his skull to the back of his head. He was about five foot ten tall and very thin with short black hair. She would never forget the bastard. She knew what Ms. Tapp looked like and where she lived.

Ms. Tapp applied the makeup and told her to smile and pose for the camera.

Bridgette put on a show for them while thinking about stabbing both of them. They would pay for this.

"Phil, what do you think I'll get for her? She is the best so far and the most risk. I'll never take one so close to home again, but she sort of fell into my lap."

"I agree, she is beautiful and thanks for the free samples. She will go for $50,000 maybe more. She could go for a lot more if the Arabs start a bidding war like on that girl from Owensboro. I made "$25,000 myself, for the handling fee. Yes, this one might top a $100,000."

"Bidding starts in five minutes so we will quickly know what she is worth."

"I'm shutting down my basement and scrubbing it clean. Do you still have the name of the guy who can make houses go away?"

"Yes, but don't do it if you just bumped up your insurance. You worried about evidence?"

"No to both, I plan well ahead and have $500,000 on the house and contents. I'm moving to Georgia to work directly for my boss down there. I don't want anything to bite me in the ass because I missed something. I also plan to pin this girl's disappearance on a dumbass that pissed me off a while back."

"I thought that you work for the school."

"I do, but I have a second job that I enjoy much more."

"Will you stay in the business?"

"Definitely. I think it's a bit too hot here with all the trouble that Jack Jr. stirred up. I know that Senior made most of his issues go away, but the jerk caused a big stink and I don't want to get caught because of him."

"Do you think his dad is involved?"

"I try not to think about him. People who even ask that question tend to disappear. I forgot that you even asked about him."

"Good."

"Hey, the bidding has started. Look $40,000 on the first bid. Damn, $100,000, $150,000, I can't keep up. This is fantastic. They love her. It slowed down at $200,000."

They waited and then the screen flashed, "SOLD for $260,000 plus a 10% auction fee."

"Girl, we are both rich. You get $260,000 and you owe me $26,000 after I deliver the girl to this rich Muslim in Saudi Arabia. Find some more like her!"

"I had another that was way hotter, but dipshit knocked her up before she killed him."

"Does your other boss know about your side business?

"Deke, if you want the job, it's yours. Jerry's recommendation sealed the deal. I will pay you $250,000 per year plus bonus and benefits."

"I accept and am very pleased to work with you and your company."

"Jerry says that you can be trusted with delicate assignments and are loyal to a fault."

"Jerry should know; I worked with him and for him for the last 10 years. I will run a top notch security group for your company and I will solve any problem that you see fit to send my way with 100% discretion."

"That's what Jerry said. Did Jerry tell you what happened to the last head of security?"

"That was an issue that Jerry asked me to handle. I trust it was handled to your satisfaction.'

"It was. The only warning that I give you is to be careful who you trust to handle my issues for you."

"The last guy was sloppy and lost his job because he trusted a couple of people who couldn't deliver and made a mess."

"With your approval, I will bring several of my own trusted people with me."

"It's your department run it as you see fit as long as Collin's Industries is protected and you successfully handle my side jobs. I already have one ongoing project that I will have my assistant bring you up to speed. It involves some criminals trying to hack into our systems. I have a team monitoring them and will need you to eliminate the threat."

"Sir to clarify, I know the adjectives delicate and eliminate."

"Good, I'll rarely use the word delicate. I handle those issues myself."

"Jack, can you break away from the office and take me to lunch today? It would make me a very happy wife and then I'll make you a very happy husband."

"Hello darling, I'm kind of busy..."

"Darling, just say Yes Dear and meet me at the club at 1:00."

"Yes Dear."

Jack Collin Sr. had his assistant move a couple of meetings, call his mistress to cancel their Monday lunch and schedule lunch with his wife. They had been married for five years and she was 15 years younger than he was. She was a former Miss Kentucky and had a Master's degree in finance from UK. She was brilliant and had taken charge of Collin's Industries foundation for charitable work which only took up a small part of her day. She wanted more.

Jack gave his wife a kiss and sat down at the table. They ordered the usual and then made small talk.

Jack laughed and asked, "I know that you didn't bring me down here to hear about your day so what gives and how much will it cost me?"

"You know how much I want a baby and I know how much that you don't want a baby. I have a suggestion for a compromise and I do believe that you will like it."

"Okay, I'll play your game. Shoot."

"Let's skip having a baby and go right to having a grandchild."

"Do what? My son is dead and I can't father children. How the hell do we...?"

"Hold on and I'll make this easy."

"Jack Jr. is about to become a father posthumously."

"What the hell are you talking about? Is that woman that he was shacked up with pregnant?"

"No she isn't, but her 15 year old daughter is pregnant and I want that baby to be ours. You get a grandchild by Jack and I get the baby that I always wanted."

"How do you know that the baby is Jack's?"

"The girl's mother tried to shake us down for some money. She was going to go to the media and tell them that Jack raped this girl and got her pregnant if we don't pay her off. I gave her a couple thousand and told her that I'd need proof it was Jack's baby before she got any more money. I was stalling until I could get you involved. We need to find out if this is Jack's baby."

"Darling, it is Jack's baby. He told me how much he loved her and that they were having sex a couple of weeks before he died. I was shocked and tried to get my son to realize that this was an underage girl when he died. I want the baby also."

Jack walked to his limo and made a call.

"This is Deke White, how may I help you?

"Very polite and business like. Deke, I was wrong. I have a delicate assignment that could turn in to eliminating a couple of issues. I know that you don't start until next week, but could you come back to the office this afternoon?"

"Sir, it sounds important. I'll be there in an hour."

"Thanks."

*

Chapter 5

Sammy was in the back yard when Grumpy brought Sam and Jeff home. When Sammy saw them, he went wild barking and trying to climb the fence. Sam led Jeff into the back yard and started playing with Sammy. They threw his favorite ball for him to fetch and then tried to play keep away by passing the ball back and forth keeping it away from Sammy. They both sat on the ground to make it fair for the height challenged dog. Sammy quickly saw that they were having fun and he didn't have a chance at capturing the ball. He went to Jeff, sat down in his lap and licked his hand. He looked up at Jeff, jumped up and licked his face. He settled down in Jeff's lap and barked for Sam to join them. She came over and sat down beside him and Sammy's tail was wagging eagerly.

"I think he likes you. Sammy is a good judge of character. We should take him to meet Ms. Tapp and see how Sammy reacts."

"Sammy growled at the name Tapp."

Jeff replied, "I don't think he likes the name Tapp."

"Sammy heard Tapp and growled again.

"Collins"

Sammy growled.

"Bill."

Tail wagging continued.

"Jack."

Sammy ran all over the yard barking and growling.

"Sam, that dog is amazing."

"I know."

Sammy ran back to Jeff and sat in his lap until GW and Kathy arrived. They went into the house, helped set the table and had another great meal.

"GW and I are going to Frankfort in the morning to talk with the Kentucky State Police to see if there are any developments in Nathan's and Gail's case. I think the three of you should keep working on the profiles and fleshing out the diagram of Collins Industries."

"Dad, we are glad to do this, but when do we get to go into the field and be real detectives?"

"Sam, I know that you are kidding, but remember that you are only 15 years old and pregnant."

"So, that was no?"

"Yes, that was no."

They went up to the room and held their own meeting. Sam was the leader and asked the other two to help her put a short list of what they knew about the murders. Both Collins and Collins Industries were on her whiteboard.

They stared at the board and Sam said, "I just had a major breakthrough."

"What is this epiphany?"

"Jeff, what does that mean?"

"Major breakthrough"

"Ok, we want to know several things to help solve these crimes. One, how did Collins get his money? Two, did he kill any of the girls himself? Three, what happened to all of the girls? There were not enough graves for all of them. Add in that we know Jack was a pedophile and Jack Sr. probably is a pedophile. Shake it up in a bag and you have the answer."

Jeff thought for a minute and said, "Are you saying that at some point Jack Sr. stopped killing all of the girls that he kidnapped and started selling them as sex slaves?

"Bingo."

Kathy thought for a second and said, "Ewwwwww! That's so gross that I can't get my mind to think about it."

"Girls it makes sense. There has always been an illegal sex trade in the world. He obtained the girls for nothing and sold them for thousands of dollars. The internet came along and he started selling them around the world. It explains the sudden wealth and early growth of Collins Industry."

"Now how do we prove it? These perverts are going to be very careful and spying on them will be almost impossible. If it were easy the cops would be able to shut them down?"

"Kathy, we have to do the drudge work first and build the profiles for the missing girls while Jeff follows the money through the internet. Jeff, while you are searching, pay attention to where Collins worked and what buildings he rented or owned. He wouldn't keep the girls at his house."

"I wonder if he just used the cabin since all of the girls are buried there. I wonder if we should go there and see what's left in the basement, garage and shed. I heard dad mention that the police were only going through the motions with the investigation. He said that the fix was in and that he heard that everything was quickly pinned on Jack Jr. and there was no reason to look further."

"Ok let's finish the profiles then we'll figure out how to go to the cabin without GW and Grumpy finding out."

Kathy and Sam continued researching the info on the girls while Jeff kept after Collins Industries. The girls had profiles on an Excel spreadsheet for over a hundred missing girls covering the area within a hundred and fifty miles of Newton. Kathy ran a pivot table and started seeing many similarities for the kidnapped girls. Most were 15-16 years old, 5 foot six inches tall, blonde hair, blue eyes and came from troubled or broken homes. Most were in the system and many were wards of the state and placed in foster homes. There was no crusade to find them by worried parents. The police searched for them for a short time and then classified them as runaways. The twenty girls identified out of the more than thirty from the cabin matched the profile. Abusive or drugged out parents and no family members to come to their rescue.

Kathy and Sam were reviewing the spreadsheets when Jeff yelled, "Eureka, I found a bunch of big cash payments!

The payments are from a bank account in New York from Lassie Studio LLC. I found their parent company, US Trading Corp Inc., based in Medford, Oregon. Wait there is another holding company and it is Bin Baden Inc., based in Saudi Arabia. The checks range from $25,000 to $250,000 and each has a reference to how many units were delivered."

"What's the date of the oldest check?"

"They only have records back to July, 30 1985. It was for $250,000 and noted 10 units delivered"

"Collins bought a small manufacturing company and an older apartment building in Louisville later that year."

"Girls, the next deposit is for $200,000 and is in October they appear to be deposited more frequently after that."

"Jeff wait a minute, we have all seen Collins in the news and those campaign adds, how old is he? He looks mid-fifties. Collins Industries got its start in the early 60s. To be buying houses in the early 60's would make him about 70-80 years old."

"Darn, you are right. What the heck is going on here? Here is his profile from Louisville's Who's Who. He was born in 1956 and his father is Jack Collins Sr. Holy crap there were three Jack Collins and I'll bet the first Collins started kidnapping the girls."

Jeff frowned and said, "It's a family tradition."

Sam asked, "Is the original Jack Collins still alive?"

"Wait a minute; I'm a few seconds ahead of you. There is a section on him and he was born on December 31, 1931. He would be in his eighties now. We need to fill GW and Mr. Jones in on this."

"Dad, we need to show you some information on Jack Collins Sr. and his money trail."

"I was just coming up to tell you to shut down for the night. It's 9:00 on a school night and Jeff's parents will be looking for him any minute. Jeff, call them and tell them I'll have you home in a few minutes."

"Yes sir."

While he called his parents, Sam told Grumpy and GW, "We found that Collins Sr. came into a fortune somehow in the sixties and invested in real estate. Then later money came from a holding company in Saudi Arabia in the 80s, but then it appears to be coming in from many different companies based all over the world."

They looked at the print outs and GW said, "So Jack Collins Sr. bought houses when he was about 6 years old with money from Saudi Arabia?"

Grumpy chimed in with, "What was he selling to these international companies. Oh, crap! It's the girls! But his age?"

"Dad, there are three Jack Collins. The grandfather was born in 1931. The current Jack Collins Sr. was born in 1956 and took over the family business. Jeff is going to continue searching their family tree to see what pops out, but this keeps getting weirder."

"Thanks guys, this is crucial information. GW and I need a day or so to process it and develop a plan. Thanks."

Grumpy took Jeff home and discussed the case on the way, "Jeff, how do you get info on old bank checks?"

"Mr. Jones, I don't think that you want to know."

"Jeff, we are fighting a war with someone, and I think it's Collins. I can't ask you do what you are doing, but I won't get in your way either. I just don't want you to get in trouble or to draw attention to the rest of us. Can you tell me that won't happen?"

"Mr. Jones, my digging on the internet is only as safe as your security guy says it is. Oh, I can misdirect them and use a bunch of servers around the world, but a good IT security guy can find me. Double check with your man and then tell me what to do."

"Thanks for explaining the situation. I'll check in the morning. Now, any luck with Sam?"

"Yes, she is warming up to me and I really like her a lot."

"Are you sure that the baby isn't a problem?"

"I wanted to date her before she got pregnant and still care a lot for her. Yes I'd rather she not be pregnant by Jack, but isn't it true that most women have dated or been married to someone else before they date or get married?"

"Yes and are you sure that you're not 35? You are very mature for a 17 year old."

"Thanks. I have always been blessed with what my dad says is plain old common sense."

"Your mom and dad should be proud of you."

"They are as I am of them. They have worked hard and sacrificed to send me to all of those extra classes. I do appreciate their support and will pay them back by succeeding in whatever I decide to do in life."

"Do you have a car?"

"No, my parents can't afford one and my money from my part time jobs go to my extra classes."

"Well if you don't mind, I'll loan you Sam's car to take her out in when you get to that point."

"Thanks very much, I was worried about that. I can always take my Dad's car, but they only have the one. Sam told me that y'all were going to build her a truck."

"We are, but I am going to give her Johnny's Mustang to drive until we get the truck built. Her birthday is in a couple of months and I want to finish my truck before we get knee deep in building hers."

"Wow, I remember that red Mustang. That is one of the most beautiful cars on the road. Sam will love it and I won't spoil your surprise."

"Thanks, I was just going to ask you to not mention our conversation."

"I won't."

The drive to Frankfort was just a little less than an hour and gave Grumpy a chance to talk with GW."

"What do you think about Jeff?"

"He seems like a nice kid. He is so polite and so smart that it is almost scary. He can't take his eyes off Sam. I'm still surprised that a teenage boy would be attracted to a pregnant girl."

"You took the words out of my mouth. I asked him about the pregnant part and he gave me a very mature answer about most women have had boyfriends or children before men start dating them."

"Wow, very mature for a teen age boy."

"Changing the subject, the two investigators that we are visiting today are Sgt. Rickards and Lt. Needmore. They are the ones who grilled me about my cop friends who were killed. Both appeared to want to solve Andy's murder and Joe's disappearance. They told me that a taskforce was to be dedicated to finding those responsible."

"Has anyone from the taskforce interviewed you or anyone that you know?"

"No and no. Have you ever run into someone with this much clout that they can shut down an investigation of a cop killer?"

"No, but remember it seems like a lifetime to you, but it's only been a couple of weeks since Andy died and everyone thinks that was an accident except you."

They arrived at the KSP Headquarters and a receptionist got them coffee and had them wait in a meeting room for about 15 minutes before Lt. Needmore appeared."

"What can I do for you two today?"

Grumpy jumped in and said, "Well you can start by giving us an update on the investigations of Andy Cox's death, the disappearance of Joe Richards and the Coles disappearance."

"The investigation of the Cox deaths was ruled an accident so the investigation was closed. I can't give you any detail on the Richards' case since it is an open case. The Coles disappearance again is an active case. We have had no new leads since the day they were abducted."

GW said, "Then please direct us to the task force looking into Richards' disappearance and the detective in charge of my son and his wife's kidnapping."

"I'm in charge of the cases for Cox and the Coles; I just gave you the only update that you will get. Lt. Holton is the officer in charge of the Richards' case and he is on vacation for the next two weeks."

Grumpy stood up and said, "So Collins has...," but GW interrupted with, "Thank you Mr. Needmore. I see that a cop killer can get away with killing cops in Kentucky and y'all just don't give a shit. I'll tell you right now, y'all better get your asses in gear and solve my son's case or you will personally have to deal with me and the national news."

"Gentlemen, you had better shut up now or I'll have you arrested for making threats."

GW stepped in the doorway and asked the receptionist to enter the room, "I want this message to go to the head of the KSP. I want a detailed report on my sons' case by 10:00 am Monday or I'll be on national media asking why Kentucky doesn't take cop killing and my sons' kidnapping seriously. Y'all may be afraid of this Collins bastard, but I guarantee you Fox News will run this story. Come on Bill let's get out of this cesspool."

GW was cursing all of the way to the truck. He finally slowed ten minutes into their drive back to Newton.

"GW, I'm glad we kept that low key and didn't poke the bear any back there. You know Collins will come for us now."

"Grumpy, you are right, but they have dropped the cases and we can't live on fear for the rest of our lives.

Sometimes you have to get the information out to the media just to insure the bad guy won't harm you. We need to get the story out on as many TV stations and newspapers as possible before he hears about our meeting."

"GW, he has already heard about the meeting. We need to watch out from now on. I'm pulling over. There are two shotguns and an AR-15 behind the seat. Get them out and keep them handy. God is looking over us, but sometimes he likes people to help themselves."

Grumpy called Mary and said, "Mary, the meeting didn't go well. We think some of the KSP are either working for Collins or are scared of him. We stirred them up and Collins may try to shut up. Keep your arms nearby and warn Martha."

GW looked at Grumpy and said, "Look man, I am so sorry. I went in there hoping that you would keep your composure. When that bastard acted like my son and Gail's disappearance wasn't worth his time to investigate I blew my top. I'm sorry if I put y'all in danger."

"I have been thinking all along that Collins was just waiting for the investigations to die down and then he would send a hit squad for us. They would fake a car wreck and make it look like an accident. Now we need to keep pushing and force him to make a mistake. We probably need to have the girls sleep in the safe room."

"Grumpy, I really stirred things up; perhaps we all need to sleep in the safe room."

"Deke, it's Corporal Lewis over at the KSP headquarters. He was Ray's contact with the KSP. Do you want to talk with him?"

"Yes, put him on through."

"Hello, I called for Ray."

This is Deke White. Ray left Collins Industries and I am now the head of security. What can I do for you?"

"Ray was interested in certain information from the KSP Headquarters. We had an arrangement."

"Why don't we assume that I am interested in the same information and perhaps anything that you hear about my new company. I'll make the same arrangement with you, if you pass on info worth having."

The corporal passed on what had been heard in the hallway between GW and Lt. Needmore plus an update on the lack of progress on two cases plus informing him that the Cox case was closed."

"Thanks, where do I send my gratitude?"

"Mr. Collins thanks for seeing me on short notice."

"Have a seat. I hope you are finding everything that you need and settling in to your new job."

"Yes, the normal security operations are going very well and the small issues were in my report yesterday. This concerns some information from my informant at the KSP. It involves someone threatening to go to Fox News about the Cox, Richards and Cole cases."

"I trust that you can eliminate this issue before it gets on the news and handle it as un-newsworthy as possible. One additional complication is that Mr. Jones foster girl, Sam, is not to be harmed."

"Thanks, that's what I have put in motion and will assure the safety of the girl. You have a nice day."

Deke knew that the same issues had been the downfall of the last security manager and he would not fall into the same trap. His men weren't on board yet, so he would call Jerry for help. He had given the problem some thought and knew he had to eliminate all of the troublemakers in one accident so well planned that even the media would broadcast it was a tragic accident. The information provided by Mr. Collins, the news media and his snitch at the KSP all pointed to Bill Jones being the major issue with GW Cole joining in just in the past few days.

Jerry's team consisted of ex-Navy Seals, Army Special Forces and a couple of corrupt ex-FBI agents. He worked with each of them for 5-10 years executing missions ranging from the rescue of kidnapped rich and famous to stealing from banks in Iraq just before ISIS invaded a town. Deke also took on assassinations if the money was in the six figures. Working for Collins would be his day job while he kept his illegal operations in full gear. After all, he had to show legitimate income to the IRS to explain his nice house, sports car and sailboat.

"Jerry, how are you doing you old goat? I have a big job and I want you to run it for me."

"I'll skin your goat if you keep insulting me. So your new boss asked you to end his issues and you want me to make sure that I don't come to end you if you fail."

"Look, we both know that you are the go to guy for him and I don't have my team in place. I want a plan that when executed eliminates the threat and everyone is standing around saying, *They were such nice guys, too bad they had an accident.*"

"How long do we have?"

"That's the rub. There is a threat to go to major media by Monday if the problem child doesn't get his way. I heard that the KSP will give him the report and that will buy us some time until he figures out that the report is BS."

"So we have five days to develop and execute the plan on the short end and a couple of weeks at the most. I'll fly in to Louisville tonight and I'll bring my own my own men. Do you have surveillance on the targets?"

"Yes, but we can't get close to them at their homes. They have a top notch security system keeping us from tapping their phones or hacking into their computers."

"So we take them away from home. Piece of cake. Can you get tracking devices on their vehicles?"

"Yes, but the target appears to be sweeping the vehicles for bugs and tracking devices every morning."

"Fill me in when I get there. This is a tough nut, but everybody makes mistakes. By the way, I want twice my usual fee due to the timing."

"Not a problem. You are the best and I don't want to end up like Ray."

"Good thinking."

Deke turned off his iPhone and thought for a minute about Jerry, *"Would Jerry kill his best friend for over 10 years. He knew the answer. Yes if the money was enough."*

*

Chapter 6

She saw Phil slip the powder in her drink as he placed the paper cup on the tray with her sandwich. She took the tray and ate her sandwich while pretending to swallow the drink. When they looked away, she poured a little at a time behind her pillow. She was certain they were drugging her and shipping her off to the man who paid for her. She made up her mind that she would die before she made that trip. She watched Phil talk with Ms. Tapp and noticed that he had a bulge under his shirt in the middle of his back at the belt line. He had a concealed gun.

Bridgette noticed that they kept looking at her and it dawned on her that they were waiting for her to pass out. She yawned, propped her head on her hand, dropped the rest of her sandwich and lowered her head onto the table.

"Check on her."

Jack walked over and rubbed her ear. She only moved her head slightly and pretended to be asleep. Phil pinched her and she didn't flinch.

"She's out and ready to move. Let's get her to the car. The flight is in two hours."

"Phil, call me after they accept the merchandise. Here's ten grand now and after the money is transferred, I'll transfer the rest of your money to your account."

"Damn, for a small girl she's hard to carry. Grab her legs and help me get her in the backseat."

They shoved and pulled her into the back seat of the Explorer and Phil got in the driver's seat and backed out of the driveway. Bridgette knew that she couldn't wait until they got to the airport to make her move, so she gagged herself and vomited. Phil quickly pulled off the road to check on her.

"Look bitch, I don't need you puking on my leather seats."

He pulled her up to a seated position and tried to see what was wrong with her. She reached behind him, gently lifted his shirt and grabbed the pistol. She shot him twice and he fell on top of her. She shoved him off and got out of the car. A few cars past, but all they saw was a girl standing by a SUV stretching her legs. She waited until there were no cars and pushed him into the back seat. He was covered in blood and so were his precious leather seats.

She pulled his wallet out of his pants and found his credit cards and over a thousand dollars in cash. She remembered that Ms. Tapp had given him ten thousand dollars and searched for it. She found a briefcase in the back of the Explorer and found the money, a Ruger MKIII with a

74

silencer, and some fake ID's with his face on them. She also saw a suitcase and found his clothes. She slipped her bloody blouse off, pulled one of his T-shirts on and then put on a light windbreaker. She slid the 1911 Colt .45 in her belt and covered the body with some of his clothes, sat down behind the wheel and drove off.

She kept checking her mirror to make sure that the police weren't following her. She felt no remorse at all for killing this scumbag who had probably sent a hundred girls into slavery around the world. She had to make a plan and get away from Newton and not be recognized. She needed to stay close enough to come back and kill Ms. Tapp, but far enough away to not be caught. She decided to drive over to Lexington and get a hotel for the night. It was a short drive, but long enough for reality to set in. She had just killed a man and had his body in the back seat. The body needed dumping somewhere hard to find until she was out of town. She also had to ditch the car and get another before the cops pulled her over looking for Phil. A thousand thoughts went through her mind and the time quickly passed.

Seeing a strip mall on the left, she pulled into the parking lot. She peeled off three hundred dollars in twenties from Phil's wallet and went into the store. She grabbed a cart, headed to the cosmetics, picked up just the basics plus some hair color, then to clothing and selected an inexpensive pair of jeans, two blouses, a bra and some underwear. As an afterthought, she found a small canvas travel bag and a purse and headed to the checkout. The clerk paid her no attention and rang up the sale. She paid and walked back to the car and drove away.

She knew she wanted a cheap hotel with very few customers in case she needed to bribe the person checking her in. Looking at her face in the mirror, she thought she could pass for eighteen so ID would not be necessary. She pulled into the Shade Tree Motel just off New Circle Road and drove around it to look into the office. Seeing just what she wanted, a skinny kid at the front desk half-asleep. She parked, walked in and saw that the boy was asleep so she hit the bell several times and startled him out of a deep sleep.

He looked up at her, smiled and almost fell off his stool.

"Mam, what can I do for you?"

She glared at him and replied, "Is this a hotel?"

He looked puzzled and replied, "Yes Mam, it is."

"Well then I want a room. Is that not what hotels do? Rent rooms, that is?"

"How long do you want the room?"

"Three days."

I'll need your credit card or you'll have to pay in full for the three nights and one hundred dollars deposit to cover any incidental charges.

She reached in her pocket to pull out the cash and felt one of his credit cards. She took it and passed it on to the clerk.

"Please fill out the info for our records," mumbled the clerk.

She freaked out for a second and wrote Kathy Cole, 100 Mockingbird Lane, Newton, Ky.

The clerk said, "You didn't write your make, model and license number for your car."

He looked out the window and said," Ford Explorer, 2012 and wes-098," and wrote the info on the document.

He swiped the card, gave it back to her with the receipt and said, "I hope that you enjoy your stay with us."

She freaked out again that there was a record of Phil's car being at the hotel. She couldn't do anything about it now, but knew she had to do better in the future. She drove around the back of the hotel to her room, went in and placed everything on one of the beds. She stripped her clothes off, took a shower and collapsed in the bed too exhausted to think about the day's events.

"Why didn't you call me about the transfer of the money for the package?"

"Phil never showed up with the package. I called him several times and he never answered his phone. The customer is very mad and this is a guy that you don't want mad at you. I'm not taking the fall for not delivering the package. You'd better get your ass in gear and find Phil."

"Why didn't you call me when he didn't show up?"

"I only deal with Phil. I don't know you. You are a person on the other end of the phone. I know Phil."

He hung up on her.

Ms. Tapp thought through all of the reasons that Phil hadn't made it to the airport and decided not to panic. She started down the normal list of who to check with if someone doesn't show up on time. She called his phone several times and just got voice mail; she the local hospitals to no avail and decided not to call the police. She called a private investigator out of Louisville that had worked for Phil before and got his voice mail. She left a message and her number.

She was frantic about the potential to lose the sale and have someone gunning for her so she jumped in her car and drove towards the airport in the chance that Phil was broke down on the side of the road. She drove around until she had to get back home and get ready to go to school.

As she was driving to school her only thought was that she had to find a replacement for Bridgette and give the girl to the Saudi customer for free to keep her reputation.

Bridgette slept in until 10:00 am, showered, colored her hair black and put on her new clothes. She had selected clothes more like a 30-year-old woman would wear in hope that they would make her look older. She didn't want every clerk and cop questioning her age. She was making mental notes on her tasks for today while she applied her make up. She knew that she had to buy a different car, get rid of the Explorer and the body, but she really needed an ID that had her age above 21. She knew that several kids in her school had mentioned a guy that sold them fake ID's so they could buy beer. She would check with him first thing today.

Just before she walked out of her room, she stopped and checked herself out in the full-length mirror. She saw a mysterious looking hot chick in tight Levis, tight blouse and pushup bra. She knew that boys thought that she was good looking, but this was a woman looking back at her. She opened her purse, got her sunglasses and put them on. Now she was glamorous and could be the woman on a magazine cover. She picked up the .45 off the dresser and placed it in her purse as she left her room.

There was a Pancake House across the street from the hotel so she walked through the parking lot and across the street to have breakfast. She noticed that several men were turning their heads and following her with their eyes as she walked. She added a little extra swing to her hips to give them a thrill.

She thought, *"Maybe I am worth a lot of money, but how do I put it in my pocket? I won't sell myself and I don't have any skills."*

She walked into the restaurant, seated herself and ordered the pancake special while she watched people come and go. There were drug dealers, people on vacation and cops eating just feet from her. She wondered if the cops' eyes were open because the drug sales were obvious. Then she decided that the cops were probably on the take to look the other way. One dealer had a big wad of cash and sat there while others brought him thick envelopes. She was beginning to have ideas about how she could make a living and perhaps get rich, but first she had a score to settle with Ms. Tapp. Several cops smiled at the drug dealer as they left the restaurant.

She paid for breakfast and walked about a mile to the bar where the guy who sold fake ID's worked.

"Is Ricky around?"

"Who wants to know?"

"Tell him that he doesn't know me, but I need his help."

The guy behind the bar took one look at her and said, "He'll want to see you. What do you drink?"

"It's a bit early, but I'll have an Apple Martini."

"That's a pussy drink; I thought you were a real woman."

Bridgette just glared at him through her sunglasses and didn't respond.

Bridgette had never been in a bar before and watched everyone to make sure that she didn't make any childish mistakes. She slowly sipped her drink and kept to herself. When in doubt, just act stuck up and shut up was her new motto. The guys ate it up and she wouldn't show how inexperienced that she was.

A guy came out of the back room and said, "Hello beautiful; what can I do for you?"

"Well first let's go to your office for some privacy."

He took her to the back room and offered her a chair and they both sat down. He offered her a beer and she shoved it away.

"I'm here on business and it's a bit early for that. I was told you are the man to help me disappear. I need a full set of ID papers. I want a driver's license, birth certificate and SS card."

"Look doll, I can get you a fake driver's license for a hundred bucks, but the others will cost some real cash."

"Look, I have a boyfriend beating me up every day and I need them. How much?"

I can get you something that will stand up for a thousand dollars cash. These will pass any inspection and you could even draw Social Security in 40 years. I can have them in two days. I need five hundred dollars up front."

She gave him the $500 dollars and said, "What's to prevent you from taking my money and not giving me my ID?"

"Nothing but my honest face."

"I'll be back in two days."

"Look doll, I know that you have thought this through, but you'll have to stop using your credit card or he will be able to trace you."

"Do I give you a new name and age?

"No, I'll tell them to find a social security number from a dead female who would now be 22 -28 years old."

"Is that how old I look to you?"

"Doll, you could be 17 to 30 with all the makeup and stuff women do to their faces. I would guess 22 and the black hair looks fake. You need a lighter color to go with your fair skin. You are so gorgeous that you should be a model."

He turned and looked in a locker and brought her a darker blonde wig for the photo for her driver's license.

She smiled and left. She was mentally kicking herself for being so stupid. She needed to use the cards for one large purchase and then burn them.

While she waited for the ID's she drove Phil's car to Henderson, KY, parked it deep into some woods by the Ohio River and wiped it clean. She walked to a gas station, called a cab and went to the bus station. She bought a ticket to Atlanta, but got off in Nashville and hitched a ride to Bowling Green, KY, where she took a bus back to Lexington. She knew she might be going overboard, but she did not want to be caught. She went back to the hotel and walked into the lobby to get a newspaper before she went to her room. The first thing she did after entering her room was to color her hair to match the photo on her new driver license.

She couldn't understand why Phil's disappearance wasn't front-page news and all over the TV. Then she remembered that he was a crook. Crooks don't report crooks missing. She hated all bad people who preyed on others like the ones who were selling her to the highest bidder. She would make them all pay and earn a living while ridding the earth of this trash and no one will call the police.

The time passed and she collected her ID's and then went to a seedy looking car lot on Russell Cave road.

"She looked at several of the cars and wanted a five year old Mustang, but knew to avoid flashy cars. She settled on a dark blue 2009 Explorer XLT. They were asking $8,000.

A sales man approached her and said, "Mam, I saw you eying that Mustang. I can make you a squeal of a deal on it and you can drive it home today."

"I'd like to test drive that blue Explorer. Get the keys if you want to sell it today."

They drove it out on New Circle road and she drove all the way around the city coming back to the car lot."

"It drives ok and I like it. Now give me that squeal of a deal."

The salesman smiled and said, "Now little lady I can knock off $200 dollars since you don't have a trade in. Let's go in and sign the papers."

"I'm not your little lady and can get this SUV for $1,500 less down the street. It has 99,000 miles and needs a set of tires. I'll pay $6,500 cash for it right now. Do you take a credit card?"

"Now wait a minute. You said cash then changed to a credit card. I have to charge more for a credit card. I'll take $6,800 on the credit card and $200 cash. The extra $300 will cover the tax and licensing fees. That is unless you want to go to the County Clerk's office and do it yourself."

"Okay deal, but I know that you'll pocket the cash."

"A man has to make a living."

He took her driver's license, typed her info on to the license application, filled out a few other forms and gave her the keys.

"Now Anna Butcher, you enjoy your new car. Oh, by the way, where do I send the plate and paper work?"

She hadn't thought about that and said, "How long will it be before they are sent?"

"Two to three weeks. Your temporary tag is good for a month."

"I'll stop back by and pick them up."

"Good luck and you're not the first house wife who escaped a wife beater. I'd change ID's and get rid of this car as soon and you can. Don't leave a trail."

She smiled, waived and sped off the lot. She had accomplished all of her tasks, but one and she thought, *"My new name fits my last task and my new job. I'll take his advice, but need some more money."*

She drove back to the hotel and took inventory of the money, credit cards and weapons. She still had over $9,000 cash, four credit cards two pistols and ammunition for both guns. One was a Ruger MK III in .22 caliber and the other was a 1911 Colt .45. There was a black tube in the briefcase and she finally figured out that it was a silencer for the Ruger. She remembered seeing one used by a guy on TV. He was an assassin. The gun made almost no noise and was deadly at close range. The man shot the guy in the head and calmly walked away.

She checked out of the hotel, loaded up her gear and drove to a mall to buy some nicer clothes and luggage. She shopped at three different stores so that she wouldn't bring attention to herself as she purchased the best clothes, shoes and accessories that they had to offer. She also purchased several high quality wigs in four different colors and lengths.

The sales lady at the last store offered her a glass of wine and said, "Are you a model or an actress? With a face and body like you have, you must be someone famous."

She sipped the wine and replied, "I'm nobody now but one of these days you will see me on TV. I have a rich husband who is in the business."

Before she left the mall, she cut up all four of the cards and flushed them down a toilet. Then she paid cash for an iPad, laptop and an iPhone all registered in her new name.

She put on much darker make up, a short brown wig and placed some latex gloves in her purse. She walked to the Pancake House about an hour before the thug normally left the restaurant. She ordered breakfast and watched as a parade of men and women sat down with the thug and passed envelopes under the table. He was a tall fat white guy with a suit on with no tie. She saw him pay his bill and get up to go. She laid a twenty on her table and followed behind him. When she got outside, she slipped the gloves on and went to the other side of his car drawing the .45 as he unlocked the car.

She opened the car door, keeping the gun hidden by her side and said, "Big boy, how about some fun?"

She sat down beside him as he said, "Mamma, you are one hot chick, but I don't do whores. Now get out of here before I pitch your ass out the window."

She pointed the .45 at him and said, "If you want to live, take a left out of the parking lot and turn right on Russell Cave Road."

The thug replied, "Do you know who you are screwing with."

"A dead man if you don't do what I say. There is a sniper with a rifle aimed at you in case I don't kill you quick enough. Your cash is not worth your life. We don't care about you, just your money. Now take your left hand and pull your gun out slowly with your thumb and one finger and pitch it in the tall grass beside your car."

He complied and drove out of the lot then turned on Russell Cave Road.

"Now turn in the parking lot of the warehouse on the left and drive around the back side of the building."

He followed her instructions.

"Now park between those stacks of pallets. See that tree to your left; there is a sniper with you in his sights. Give me all of the envelopes and if you pull a hidden gun, you die. I'll shoot you or the sniper kills you."

He reached into his coat and pulled the envelopes out a couple of bundles at a time. The suit had numerous hidden pockets containing over twenty envelopes.

She smiled at him and said, "Do you run prostitutes?"

He laughed and she shot him three times. He was too late reaching for his hidden gun. She picked it up and shot several bullets into the car to confuse the police. She placed the envelopes in her purse and calmly walked away from the car and went on around the building and down the street several blocks to her car.

The drive to Owensboro only took a couple of hours on highway 64, but was long enough to allow her to think through what she had to accomplish. She had over 30 thousand dollars from the robbery of the drug dealer plus about three thousand left from Phil's money. Now she wanted to find a nice apartment or house to rent so she had a base of operations and more pressing, she had to have an address for to obtain a credit card and bank account. She made up a story about being recently divorced and had alimony to cover her expenses. She wanted to rent from an individual so there would be no challenge with all of those forms and references. She picked up the usual apartment and home finder magazines and went to a nice restaurant for lunch and to see what was available. She ate lunch while looking through the magazines.

She noticed that all of the men were checking her out as they came and went to their tables. This made her feel very good about herself. The dirty perverts had no idea that they were checking out a sixteen-year-old girl.

She found four apartments and two homes, furnished, for rent by owner. She called the owners of two apartments and the homes to make appointments for that afternoon. She continued to work on her story about marring an abusive rich man and moving into his house, but after a couple of beatings, she got a divorce so she had only her clothes and personal items. She didn't like the apartments and the first house, but the last house was very nice and in a decent neighborhood.

The rent was steep at $1,200 per month, but she wanted it and the utilities except cable were included.

"Mam, why are you renting your house?"

"I kept it in my divorce and my husband moved in with his secretary. I just married a wonderful man and decided to keep my house. The house is the only thing that I own, besides my car. The house is paid for and the rent minus upkeep will be my own money. I need the first's month's rent now and a thousand dollar security deposit."

"Is cash ok? As I mentioned I have just split with my husband and am starting over. I emptied our checking account and have to live on that until the alimony starts next month. I get it for five years and will go back to school to finish my degree at KY Wesleyan and then worry about a job. Richard was very wealthy, but abusive. He will pay for that for the next five years. Can you recommend a good bank?"

"I was lucky; my husband just cheated and never beat me. I would have killed his sorry butt if he ever laid a hand on me."

She took the cash, gave Anna a receipt and recommended a local bank.

"I'll be moving in after I finish a few tasks in Louisville. Thanks so much for sharing your nice house with me."

"The rent is due on the 1st and here is my phone number and the number of the guy that does any repairs on the house. You'll have to mow the grass or pay someone. I've included a good lawn care company on the list."

She thanked the lady and went into her new home. She got her laptop out, pulled up a map of the area and noticed that Nashville, St. Louis, Indianapolis and Louisville were only a short drive from Owensboro. She could easily apply her new trade in those cities and live in Owensboro. The bad guy will be dead and the cops won't be called.

Before she headed back to Newton she stopped by Independent Bank, opened a checking account and applied for a credit card. She only deposited $5,000 because she was afraid a larger deposit would raise eyebrows. She then traveled to two more banks, started bank accounts with them and deposited the same amounts. She was pleased with herself. She had checked off all of her tasks and being an adult was easy so far.

She went back to her new house and made a list of everything that she would need to purchase for her new home. She went shopped for cooking utensils and bought a large gun safe at Rural King. She had it delivered and installed in the garage. She wanted a safe place to store her cash while she figured out how to deposit it in a bank without drawing suspicion. She also bought several boxes of .22 and .45 auto ammunition. She mentioned to the clerk that they were for her boyfriend. She later drove to Henderson and Evansville, Indiana to purchase the rest of her needs. She spread out her cash purchases in all three towns.

Her home was stocked. She had the gun safe and the ability to protect herself. She knew that what she didn't know would bite her in the butt so she spend several hours each day searching the internet and even watched several crime movies to make sure that she wasn't missing anything. She quickly found out that she needed car insurance, renter's insurance, firearms training and a home security system. She called the landlord and got permission to have the system installed.

She was ready to go see Ms. Tapp.

*

Chapter 7

Sam, Kathy and Jeff took lunch together outside on the grass away from the others so they could compare notes on the Collins' investigation.

"Sam, I've exhausted everything I know to look up on Collins and Collins Industries. We are at a standstill until we can search the area around the cabin or have another breakthrough."

"Jeff, what if we speak to the people who have been scared off by Collins? Let's make a list of the ones that are known and then see if we can find others."

Both Kathy and Jeff thought that was a good idea, but Kathy spoke up and said, "My friend Bridgette is still missing and no one is looking for her. If we don't find her soon, she will disappear forever."

Sam quickly agreed and asked, "How do we even start searching for her?"

Jeff said, "Does anyone else know she is missing? Let's tell the police what we know and get them started. They deal with this all of the time. Then at the same time we can figure out how to search for her on our own."

"Jeff, you are so good at this. You never look over anything. We should report her missing today."

"I'll call Gramps and get him to take me by the police station after school while y'all figure out how to begin the search. I'll see y'all later."

Kathy was excited about getting the police to begin searching for Bridgette. She called GW and he agreed with starting with the police.

He picked Kathy up after school and apologized as soon as she got in the car.

"Kathy, I'm a cop and I should have thought about your friend and reporting her missing. My only defense is that I have been worried to death about your mom and dad."

"Gramps, I did the same thing. The important thing is to get the police looking for her before they take her out of town. I want to post her picture and a reward for information leading to her return. Can we afford some money?"

"Kathy, if it is a sex ring, she is probably a thousand miles from here. Don't mention Collins, Senior or Junior. Let me think about how much for a reward. Too much and you get a million fake calls, too little and no one calls. Put an example together and we'll go from there."

91

"I know Gramps; we don't want to piss off the Collins."

They told the officer at the front desk they were there to report a missing person and were led to a conference room.

In a few minutes, an officer entered the room, "I'm Sgt. Wills and I hear you want to report a missing person. Aren't you the girl with the missing parents?"

"Yes she is and I'm her Grandfather, but this is about one of her friends at school."

"Why haven't her parents filed a missing person's report?"

"Her mom and step-dad were murdered the other day and she has been missing ever since."

I remember that case. I'll get the file. He came back with another police officer and a file.

"Hello, I'm Lt. Black and I am handling the Weber/Payne case. Our records show that the grandparents came and took the girl back home with them."

Kathy spoke up, "Well they didn't because she only has one grandparent and she is in a rest home and doesn't know where her granddaughter is because she has dementia. Where did you hear that she went with her grandparents?"

"The notes say that her school called us to report her being pulled out of school."

"Well someone lied to you and Bridgette is missing. Several weeks before the murders and her kidnapping, she told me that she reported to Ms. Tapp at the high school that her stepdad was abusing her. She told me that Ms. Tapp said that she would handle reporting the situation. Nothing happened and then Bridgette told me that someone from the school was getting her drunk and raping her. We think that person killed her parents and kidnapped her."

"The coroner has ruled a murder–suicide for her parent's deaths and we weren't looking for the girl."

"Did you see the grandparents or Bridgette at her mom's funeral? Don't you think she would attend? Check her out and you will see that I'm telling the truth. Someone took her and killed her parents."

"Okay, I'm not promising anything, but we will reopen the case. You've brought up some issues that we didn't know about. Before you go, I need a written statement from you on what you said Bridgette told you."

Kathy wrote down everything Bridgette told her and then they left to go to Kathy's house to check on it before heading back to the Jones' house.

Sam left Jeff to go to fifth period class and made a detour to the school secretary's office.

"Hello, Mrs. Thompson, I need an address to send a card to Bridgette Payne. I believe I heard that she moved to her grandparent's home. My mom says that I should send her a sympathy card."

"Hi, Sam, how is the baby coming along? I'll get it for you. We have to send her school records there and I'll do that today after I find out what school she is attending."

Sam watched her go to a big bank of filing cabinets and then back to her desk to look at her computer."

"I'm sorry Sam. We were told she moved back to Idaho with her grandparents, but I can only find a grandmother in Maine and she is in a rest home. I'll check with Ms. Tapp and see if she has the address. Go on to class and I'll bring the address to you."

Sam went on to biology class then her sixth period English class with Jeff.

"Jeff, the school doesn't have any record of her new address. Mrs. Thompson is checking with Ms. Tapp to see if she has Bridgette's address."

"Smells rotten to me. Sam you need to be careful. Ms. Tapp may not be Collins, but she could sure cause you some trouble at school."

Just before the class ended, Sam was called to Ms. Tapp's office.

Sam walked into her office and said, "Ms. Tapp, they said that you wanted to see me."

"Yes, I heard that you are looking for Bridgette Payne's new address."

"Yes, my mom wants to send her a sympathy card."

"Well you can give me the card and I'll send it to her."

"Why can't you give us the address? Kathy Cole and I want to stay in touch with her and will be asking her for her new phone number."

"I'm sorry, but for her protection, I can't give out her address."

"Mam, why does she need protection? Is someone trying to hurt her like they killed her parents?"

Sam could see Ms. Tapp's face get redder by the second.

94

Ms. Tapp replied, "No the police just asked us not to give it out without their approval."

"Well thanks anyway. Kathy's Gramps is a homicide detective and he has a friend on the police force. He'll get it from them. Thanks and sorry for bothering you."

"Go back to your class."

The bell rung and Kathy went back to class to get her backpack and joined Jeff out front to wait on Grumpy to pick them up.

"Jeff, she about crapped her pants when I said that GW would get Bridgette's new address. She may not be the one who was abusing Bridgette, but she looked awful guilty trying to dodge my questions. We need to do a more thorough search on her this evening."

Jeff replied, "Sam, don't get me wrong, I believe that you are doing the right thing by investigating these cases, but don't you ever take a rest? I'd like to take you out on a real date one day when the crap isn't hitting the fan."

Sam laughed, "Let's take a break this afternoon and play with Sammy. I'll also listen about your plans to take me out."

Jeff held her hand and they talked until Grumpy arrived to take them home in the red Mustang.

"Dad, is this the car that's been under the tarp in your garage?"

"Sam, don't BS me. I know that you have been looking under the tarp for months. I checked it all out and got it running this morning. We are short one car and I thought your mom would want to drive it until we get her a new one. The shop called this morning and they said that her car wasn't worth fixing."

He winked at Jeff and said, "I might just trade this thing off for Mom a new car."

"Jeff, get in the back. I couldn't get my fat body back there with a crowbar. Dad, fire it up and let's see what she'll do!"

Grumpy pulled away slowly and blended in with the traffic until he got on the road that goes to their house.

He stopped and said, "Hold on, even with this weight a 427 will throw you back in the seat."

He pushed the pedal down, the tires screamed and the car took off like a rocket. He only ran it up to 60 MPH before backing off. The car ran great and even looked better. Sam wanted it. They drove on to the house and Sam wanted to sit behind the wheel. Grumpy moved the seat all of the way back and she could sit in the car, but her short legs and arms couldn't reach the pedals and steering wheel.

"Well I guess Jeff will have to drive when we go on our first date."

Grumpy winked at Jeff and said, "That'll be the day. Ya'll go give Sammy some attention. He's kept me busy fetching his ball."

They took Sammy on a walk down the road towards Jeff's house. Sammy chased squirrels and rabbits every time he saw one and would try to get Jeff to get the squirrels down after he treed them. He would pull Jeff by his pants leg to the tree then bark at Jeff to get the squirrel for him.

"Sammy, my dear boy, Jeff's not going to get that squirrel for you. Those squirrels have sharp teeth and would eat you up like a buzz saw."

Sammy ignored Sam and still begged for a squirrel. Sam reached in her pocket and pulled out a treat for Sammy. She

96

made him jump several times before she lowered the treat low enough for Sammy to get the treat. They were walking down the middle of the road when Sammy started barking and made them look behind them. A car whizzed by almost hitting both of them. It was a blue Volvo with an Obama Biden sticker on the right side of the bumper. The car never slowed down and disappeared out of sight.

"Sammy may have saved us from that maniac. Did you get a glimpse of the driver?"

"No, I was busy trying to get out of its way, but I did notice that it was a woman in a green blouse or dress. You don't think she tried to run us over, do you? Ms. Tapp had a green blouse on today and she has a blue Volvo."

"I don't know, but she sure didn't slow down to apologize. Let's walk back to your house and get to work."

"You just want some more of Mom's cooking don't you?"

"Your mom is a freaking good cook."

They were holding hands when they saw a car coming towards them. Sammy got off the road into the bushes and hid. The car got closer and it was Jeff's mom and dad coming home from work.

Jeff's mom greeted them, "Well aren't you such a good looking couple; taking little Sammy out for a walk. I saw y'all holding hands until we drove up."

"Hi Mr. and Mrs. Stone. Jeff and I wanted to take Sammy for a walk and get some exercise."

"How is the baby coming along? When are you due?"

"It's due in 10 weeks."

"You don't know the sex yet?"

"No, I wanted to be surprised. Mom and I agree on that. It would be easier to buy clothes and get the baby's room decorated accurately, but we chose not to know. Mom and I are hoping for a girl and Grum... err dad wants a boy to spoil rotten."

"Dad, did a blue Volvo pass you on the way here?"

"Yes son. Why are you asking?"

"One almost ran over us and was going at least 80 when it went by us. Sammy barked and saved us from being hit. He has great ears. It was on us just as we heard it."

"We're studying late this evening again."

His mom said, "Just make sure that's all you do."

"Mom!"

They drove off and Sam and Jeff didn't speak for a minute until Sam said, "What did she mean by that comment. What does she think we are doing?"

The question was innocent, but it put Jeff on the spot.

He looked around and said, "She meant that we shouldn't be fooling around."

"You, Kathy and I always fool around."

"You and I fooling around."

She suddenly turned red and replied, "Did she mean, don't have sex? I can't have sex. Crap, I'm already pregnant; you can't have sex when you're pregnant can you?"

"Don't ask me. I'm a teenage boy; we want sex all of the time. Well that's what our Health book says anyway. That didn't sound right, but you know what I mean."

"Well we're not doing that. It's not going to happen. Once is enough for me. Never again."

98

Jeff knew to shut up while he was behind and they walked back to the house holding hands."

Mary had cooked green beans, mashed potatoes and a salad while Grumpy grilled some pork chops for supper.

Sam said grace, "Lord, please guide us in making this world a better place and thanks for the food and the people around this table tonight. Lord please help me get through these next two months and don't let me explode like a balloon from getting so fat."

Jeff choked and everyone tried to stifle their laughter, but all failed and burst out laughing."

"It may be funny to you, but I weighed a hundred pounds fully dressed when I joined this family and I weight one hundred and forty five pounds now. I feel like a walrus. I have to have help getting up and I'm afraid I'll starve to death if I ever get left alone on my back."

They started laughing again and discussed the soon to be born baby for the rest of the meal.

They went up to Sam's room and Sam gave Kathy an update on the meeting with Ms. Tapp.

"Sam, you don't mind stirring crap, do you? She is involved in this somehow. I want to find my friend and I'm afraid that it's too late to help her. Let's drop Collins for a while and concentrate on Ms. Tapp. Jeff you handle her finances and we'll search for any information that we can on the internet."

Sam added, "Jeff you hacked into the school computers, can you get into her personnel file?"

"What do you think about posting missing person fliers all over the area? I want to post Bridgette's picture with a reward for information."

They both thought that it was a great idea and Kathy would start on it tomorrow.

Jeff turned to his laptop and in five minutes printed out five pages on Ms. Dorthea Alice Tapp.

"Girls, this looks pretty boring, but you can do a thorough search. You have her SS number, birth date and info on her Teachers Credit Union account."

The girls found all of the usual info about where she was born, her school info and the college she attended. She was born and lived in Cupperton, Georgia and both her parents worked for a CP Industries located on the outskirts of Cupperton.

"Hey Jeff, isn't there a large store in Louisville named CP Outfitters?"

"Yes, dad takes me there a couple of times a year. We buy guns, ammo, camping and fishing equipment there. It's a great store with lots of stuffed animals and a big glass tank with all types of live fish swimming around. Look them up on the internet."

Sam rolled her eyes and said, "All you talk about is sex and looking things up on the internet."

"Kathy had just taken a big gulp of sweat tea in her mouth and gave Sam a shower when she broke up at what Sam said."

Kathy ran and got some towels out of the bathroom to clean Sam up while apologizing.

"Sam I'm so sorry, but that comment was way out there. Are y'all...?

Jeff interrupted and said, "No, but that not your business. It's an inside joke."

He was turning red and his face got hotter and hotter.

Kathy started laughing and said, "You red headed white people turn all shades of red when you get embarrassed. I think red headed white people look like a fire engine going to a fire. We black folks stay black and don't change our color like a lizard."

"Yes, but you can see my face in a dark room and not just my teeth."

Kathy just stared at him and started acting as if he hurt her feelings.

She saw him turning even redder and broke out laughing, "I guess I deserved that comment, Chief Red in the Face."

Sam took some clothes to the bathroom and changed out of her soggy ones. Mary saw her coming out of the bathroom and had a puzzled look on her face.

"Mom, Kathy decided to spray me with sweat tea. We cleaned up the mess and I'll get even after Jeff goes home?"

"Don't hurt her and don't burn the house down. We're playing Hearts down in the kitchen if you need anything."

"Thanks Mom, I have to get back to work."

Jeff and Kathy were very excited when Sam came back in the room.

She asked, "What are you two doing. Plotting against me while I'm out of the room?"

"No, we found several large bank accounts in Ms. Tapp's name and they both have large sums of money going to Collins Industries and deposits from some of the same overseas companies and banks that Collins had."

"Holy crap, do y'all think that she is kidnapping and selling girls also."

"Yes, we do. It's starting to come together. Collins is a busy executive; he has to have people that work with and for him to make this international sex slave thing work. Ms. Tapp would know which girls were in trouble and wouldn't be missed."

Sam thought for a minute and asked, "How do we get into her computer at home? Do we have to sneak in and check her computer and see if she has a basement with trophies from young girls?"

"Sam, you can't mean breaking into her home, that's against the law!"

"Wait a minute Jeff, Sam was kidnapped, the Jones and Sam were attacked and my parents are missing and probably dead. The law has done nothing to solve these crimes."

"Jeff can you do a search and wipe out the trail so it can't be used against us later?"

"I can, but what are you going to research?"

"How to break into Ms. Tapp's house without getting caught. Burglars R Us."

"Okay, but what if she notices that someone broke into her house? She goes to the police and then they find us and put us in jail."

"Well, we won't take anything, we are below 18 and they won't send you to jail for a prank against a teacher. Besides, I don't think she wants the police snooping around the house; she won't call them."

"You are right. She doesn't want any publicity. She has over a million dollars in those accounts. She is definitely doing something illegal. You can't save up that much on a teacher's pay. If it were an inheritance, she'd have it in an IRA or investments. She has a pile of cash in bank accounts drawing low interest."

"Well are you going to tell me what you did to get the tea sprayed on you?" Mary asked.

Sam had just poured her cup of coffee and was looking at the sun as it rose over the trees in the back yard. No one else was up yet and it was Mary's and her special time together.

"I said something that cracked her up and she sprayed me with sweat tea. It was so funny watching her blow like a volcano, until it hit me in the face."

"Can I ask what you said or is it private?"

"Kinda private, but I trust you. It started when Jeff's mom made a comment to Jeff and me and then Kathy choked when I told her."

"Well you peaked my interest. What did Jeff's mom say?"

"His mom and dad stopped to say hi while we were walking Sammy and Jeff told her that we would be studying in my room. When they drove off she said, "Just make sure that's all you do.""

"Mary said, "She didn't know that Kathy was in the room with y'all. Why was that so funny to Kathy?""

"Mom, put your coffee cup down and swallow your coffee and I'll tell you.'

She gave Mary the detail and watched Mary turn red. Mary didn't laugh.

"Sam, did they cover sex in school?

"Not very well apparently."

They had a mother daughter talk and then they went to prepare breakfast.

"Mom, can you start teaching me how to cook and how to take care of my baby?

"Darling I already planned to help you with homemaking and caring for children. You know the best thing I can do is to set a good example as a housewife and wife to your dad. You may decide to go into business or be a lawyer, but learning to cook and be a good wife could also come in handy."

Two days later, they had gathered the equipment and knowledge together to get into Ms. Tapp's house. Grumpy dropped the girls off at school and they waited until Grumpy left before meeting Jeff at a store down the block from the school. To avoid drawing too much attention, Sam and Kathy walked to the alley behind the house by themselves and Jeff joined them a few minutes later. They hid along a fence behind some bushes while Jeff picked the lock on the back door. Sam and Kathy slipped on their latex gloves and went in while Jeff walked around to the end of the block to be their look out just in case Ms. Tapp came home early.

"Kathy, plug this device into her computer and restart the computer. It will take about 15 minutes so do it first thing then remember to unplug it and take it with you when you leave."

"Sam, you take the upstairs and I'll search the basement. We need to be out of here in thirty minutes."

Sam quickly walked through all of the rooms and settled on the office. She took her phone and took a picture of the area that she was looking at so she could put everything back in its place. She searched a large bookcase by removing books and even thumbing through many of them. She then searched the desk and found a stack of notes that had what appeared to be brief descriptions of girls. She plugged the device into a USB port and turned on the computer.

She found a note that said, *"One short skinny blonde, two tall well-built brunettes and a tall well-built blonde."*

There were checkmarks beside each description and she noticed that the last page had a checkmark by, "Tall well-built redhead." There had been a checkmark, but it had been erased.

She thought, *"Holy crap. These look like order forms for young girls."*

She took pictures of all of the pages and continued searching the desk. She found a notebook that had the letters CP on the front, thumbed through it and saw that it appeared to document conversations with someone named Bo. She saw a reference to Chosen People several times. Again, she took pictures of every page.

She thought, *"CP and Chosen People. We don't have time now, but that needs to be looked into."*

Kathy flipped the light switch on as she headed down the basement stairs. One light came on and gave her enough light to travel down the steps to the floor. She found another switch and saw the usual basement clutter. Boxes of clothes, a bicycle and magazines were stacked along the walls. She went to the back of the large room and saw a door. She opened it and turned the light on. What she saw scared her and she wanted to bolt back up stairs. She made herself go into the room even though her knees were wobbly and her heart was pounding. She saw a mattress on the floor, a table, chair and a length of chain bolted to a steel pole. She looked around and didn't see anything else until she got closer to the wall. Down close to the floor, almost blocked by the bed, there were several names scratched in the paint. One name took her breath away. **Bridgette Payne**. Tears started flowing down her cheeks as she took pictures of the wall and everything in the room. She wiped the tears from her face and headed back up stairs.

Just as Kathy walked into the office Sam's phone rang. They both jumped and their hearts raced as if they'd been caught red handed.

It was Jeff, "Hey Sam, it's been twenty five minutes. Y'all need to wrap it up and get out of there."

"Okay, we're almost done and I have the device in my pocket."

"Good girl, be careful.

Kathy and Sam quickly compared notes and walked towards the kitchen to leave through the back door. They were almost to the door when they heard the door jiggle and they saw two men through the blinds. Kathy grabbed Sam and they ran back towards the hallway. Kathy pointed to the front door and saw another man standing just outside on the porch. They were in front of the basement door and quietly walked down the dark stairs using the flashlights on their phones.

The two men came in the back door and one traveled through the hallway and opened the door for the one at the front door. The one in the kitchen had a toolbox and he started snooping around the kitchen while the others searched the house.

"This woman has screwed over the wrong man. Mahmud is not a man to mess with. Check the basement while I search the attic and Dameer finishes his work. The girl may not be here, but we had to come anyway to let Dameer perform his duty."

The man turned the light on and walked down the steps with his pistol drawn and ready. He looked around the room and quickly saw that there was no place for anyone to hide. He saw the door at the back of the room, opened it and turned the light on. He heard something move behind him and he turned and jumped when he saw the rat. He hated rats. He had been

107

in prison in Iraq for three years and rats were everywhere. He had numerous bites from the devils.

He walked back towards the door, stepped into the room and looked around. He could see that this was where she kept the girls, but there was no one there now. He turned the lights off and left the basement. Dameer had finished his work and they left through the back door.

Jeff had called several times and no one answered so he calmly walked down the street to the alley just in time to see the men walking from the back of the house and leaving in a black SUV. He called Sam again and no one answered. He ran to the back door and broke the glass to enter the house. He ran through the house and didn't see any one so he ran down the basement steps and the first room was empty. He saw the door and opened it, tripped and fell on something soft. He got up just as all hell broke loose. Someone kicked him on the shin and hit him on the chest. He grabbed an arm and threw the person to the ground just when a light flooded the room.

He had Kathy pinned down when Sam yelled, "Hey Jeff it's us. We thought you were the bad guys."

"Girls, let's get out of here, we can compare notes later."

Jeff herded them up the stairs and out the back door very quickly.

When they got into the back yard, he said, "Now slow down so we don't attract attention. They calmly walked while the girls filled him in on what had happened.

Sam told him, "We saw the men at the back and front doors and had no choice but to go down into the basement. There was no place to hide so we crawled under the mattress and hid from them. We were still hiding when you tried to kill us by jumping on the mattress."

She had just finished speaking when an explosion shook the whole neighborhood and knocked them off their feet. Jeff caught Sam and buffered her fall by letting her fall on him. Debris started raining down on top of them. A piece of brick struck Kathy and a shingle hit Jeff. They only received scratches and bruises.

Jeff hugged Sam and checked her for any cuts or wounds as he said, "Sam, are you okay? Is the baby ok?"

"I'm ok and I guess the baby is okay. Let's get away from here now."

They got up and quickly walked on down the block.

"Oh my God! Those men blew Ms. Tapp's house up."

Sam replied, "We were in that house 10 minutes ago. We could have all been killed."

They calmly walked back to school and each went to their next class. They were in class when they saw a police car pull up to the front of the school. Sam excused herself, went to Ms. Tapp's office and saw a cop talking with the principal.

"I'm sorry' but Ms. Tapp got a call and left a few minutes ago. Can I help you?"

"We just came to get her because she isn't answering her phone. Her house just blew up and destroyed the houses on either side. We are lucky that no one was home. There's just a big hole in the ground where her house used to be."

*

Chapter 8

Bridgette was just a couple of blocks from Ms. Tapp's house when the explosion shook the neighborhood. She stopped at the last cross street before the Tapp house and saw that it had disappeared and the houses around it were on fire.

She thought, "*Damn, somebody got to her before me. I'll hold up in a hotel and see if they killed the bitch. It has to be the Saudis, but it could be just a faulty furnace. I'll stick around, find out what happened and take my time dealing with that bitch. With my dishwater blond hair and fancy clothes I'm Anna Butcher and even my friends wouldn't recognize me. I'll be Anna from now on.*"

She drove off before the police and fire trucks arrived. The Homewood Suites Motel was just two miles away and she could keep an eye out for Ms. Tapp while checking the local news to see what happened at the house.

This was a nice hotel and she walked in as if she owned the place. She paid cash and made a mental note to go on line and get another credit card. She needed a personal credit card and a business one. She tipped generously and went to her room feeling as if she was 25 and wealthy. She examined the room and while it was very nice, she wanted to get enough money so that she could stay in the nicest hotels and have a mansion. She was going to be somebody and the bad guys would be her source of income.

She knew that she needed to learn a lot about how these criminals functioned and how they moved cash around. She watched several documentaries on organized crime and drug gangsters before searching the internet to learn what she could. She finally decided that she needed to find the bars and restaurants that were money drops from the drug pushers to the drug lords. That's where the cash was and she could find one to hang out in and learn. She would avoid the counting rooms and drug distribution since they were heavily armed. She decided to get several more fake ID's and use a different one for each town. She would be Anna Butcher for her private life and set up bank accounts, credit cards and at least one safe house in case something hit the fan. She would develop knowledge of the drug operations in all of the big cities on the east coast and only hit one per month in any one city.

She ordered in for supper and caught the 6 o'clock news, which had 5 minutes on the big explosion in Newton. She looked up and saw Ms. Tapp in the crowd watching the fires being extinguished by the firefighters and then a local reporter interviewed her.

Late that night she decided to drive to Memphis to test her knowledge of how to rob drug dealers. She wanted to perfect her trade as far away from her new home as possible. She wanted the situation in Newton to calm down and Ms. Tapp to start feeling comfortable in her new home before she tried to have a discussion with her.

The reporter saw her and asked, "Ms. Tapp have they told you what happened to your house?"

"No, I just came here from school after a neighbor called to tell me about the explosion."

"Have you had any furnace or water heater problems? Have you smelled any gas?"

"No and no. I have no idea what happened. I'm just like everyone else on the block and don't know a thing. This is terrible and I hate to think that my house was the cause of this horrible situation."

Ms. Tapp called her insurance agent, told her the situation and then got a hotel room. She knew that she had to disappear. The Saudis had to be responsible for trying to kill her. She couldn't sleep all night and planned to empty her bank account and head west to California. She already had fake ID's for her work with the Chosen People, but knew that if they found out about her side business that Bo would kill her. They were racists and working to overthrow the government, but they wouldn't stand for child abuse.

She finally fell asleep that night and rested peacefully knowing that she would start a new live in the Bay area. No one would miss a few girls out there and she would stay away from the Saudis.

The next morning she checked the news and found nothing new concerning the explosion. As usual, there was a lot of speculation, but no facts. She went down to the hotel restaurant for breakfast and had fruit and cereal with coffee. She was just ready to leave when two men sat down on either side of her. They were both of mid-eastern decent and wore business suits.

The one on the left said, "Ms. Tapp, did we get your attention?"

"Who are you? Leave me alone or I'll call the police."

"Ms. Tapp, you know who we are and you know that we could have blown your house up at night with you in it. If you yell or call the police, Omar will slit your throat and we will walk out of here and disappear. So listen to my offer. You now work for Sheik Amir; you will find the red haired beauty and deliver her to us. You will deliver 10 girls per month and we will pay you $25-$50 thousand per girl. If you deliver more of the ones like the red haired girl, we will double the fee. This is easy; work for us or die. What is your decision?"

"I will work for you. What do I tell the police when they start asking why a vice principal is a target of a bombing? Do you care where I live or what my name is? I may have to get out of town."

"Use your imagination and don't try to hide from us. We will find you. Use this number to contact me. We can get you new ID's and paperwork."

He handed her a card and they left; it took an hour before her heart stopped racing. She called the school and took time off to deal with her house. The principal was very understanding, but told her that he needed to discuss the Bridgette Payne situation. She agreed to a meeting the next day.

Ms. Tapp felt the noose tightening and had to come up with a way out. She would please the Saudis and make a lot of money, but she had to get past the Bridgette situation quickly. Too many questions were coming her way from the school and that brat Sam Smith. She knew what she had to do and called a friend of Phil's to help her execute her plan.

Mr. Lee was at home that evening working in his garden pruning his prize winning roses. He was a quiet man who kept to himself and visited his mom at the Daisy Hill rest home twice a week. He was the AP Chemistry and Physics teacher at the high school, went to church on Sunday and was a scout leader. He was also a peeping Tom. He used high tech gear to peer into back yards and through windows. He had the latest UAV's and could look into the girls windows and down at the swimming pools and sunbathers. He also installed tiny cameras outside of several girls' windows. He would never harm anyone and thought people shouldn't do anything they didn't want to be seen.

He had miniaturized cameras on the unmanned aircraft and had the signal sent to a DVR so he could watch the girls over and over. He rarely got more than a girl in a bikini or a fuzzy view into their bedrooms, but he was still a pervert.

Ms. Tapp knew that the police had investigated him in the past, but couldn't pin anything on him. Ms. Tapp watched as her friend picked the lock on the back door. It was midnight and there were no light on the back of the house. They entered the house, quickly found Lee's bedroom and found him fast asleep. Ms. Tapp found his laptop on the dining room table and brought up his Facebook page. She posted a couple of pictures of young girls from his classes including one of

114

Bridgette. Then she posted a suicide note saying that he knew that he was sick and had to die for what he did to Bridgette. While she was on Facebook, her friend placed some magazines with underage girls in several places around the house. He also placed a block of C4 and some electronics for bomb making in with Lee's remote control parts for his UAVs.

She found files on his computer containing films he made of many of the girls in the neighborhood and saw several that she recognized from the high school. Several were obviously filmed from outside their bedrooms. She was happy when she found pictures of Bridgette. She left them on the screen and went to join her friend.

She walked into his bedroom very slowly, one step after another, afraid that a squeaking board would wake Mr. Lee up. A fight would leave contusions and bruises that would eliminate the chance of convincing the police and a coroner that Lee committed suicide. Every squeak and noise made her heart race as she moved closer to him. She saw his face and he was smiling in his sleep. He was sleeping on his back and snoring, which probably kept him from hearing them enter his room.

Since he was the Chemistry teacher, they decided to have him poison himself with Cyanide. Her friend got a glass from his kitchen, poured the glass half full and placed the rest on his bedside table. She gently pinched his nose closed and when he opened his mouth, she poured the liquid death into his mouth. He gagged and swallowed. Her friend held his arms down with pillows to prevent bruising. He yelled and looked her in the eyes and struggled before the poison started to take effect. Her friend released Mr. Lee's arms and he lay there dying while holding his neck. He gagged, froth leaked out of his mouth and he died.

They snuck out of the house, walked to the car and left. They had worn hospital scrubs, hair nets, and gloves; there was no trace of them ever being in the house.

As they were driving back to the hotel her friend said, "I know Phil handled your logistics for you. I want that business."

She thought, "*I knew there would be a catch to getting his help.*"

"Gary, I'll give you a try and if it works, you'll get my business."

"I will take care of your needs and as you saw tonight, I can perform other services."

It was 8:00 am, when Ms. Tapp dropped in on the principal as he requested. She wanted him to hear her story before he found out about Lee's suicide.

"Hello Barry, I'd say good morning, but when your house blows up and almost destroys the entire neighborhood you don't feel very good."

"Well it's good to see you and that you weren't hurt in the explosion. Is there anything that the school or I can do for you?"

"My insurance company is taking good care of me so far. I only need to take some time to find a place to live while we sort out the house. Everything I owned except my car and the clothes on my back were destroyed in the blast."

"Take the time that you need, just stay in touch with me and don't hesitate to ask for help."

"I will, now what do you need to discuss?"

"Dot, there have been questions concerning Bridgette Payne's withdrawal from school. We can't find any records and there is just a note that you told the secretary that her grandparents had taken her back to Idaho with them."

"That's correct; I passed that on from Mr. Lee. He told me that they contacted him and asked him to pass on the information."

"Didn't you think this was odd?"

"Well now maybe; I pushed him at first and asked several questions, but their daughter had just been killed, so it didn't raise any flags when he told me the story. Lee hasn't liked me since I helped the police in that investigation of him last year. Now that I think about it, he should have gone to the admin office. I am the Vice Principal; perhaps he thought he was reporting it properly. Why, what's going on?"

"Well, we can't find where she is to send her files to her new school. The police came by, they want to know where she transferred to and we can't help them. Lee is out today, but I will catch him tomorrow. Thanks for dropping by."

She knew that Lee's friends that were checking their Facebook page were seeing Lee's last post and calling the police by now. She went shopping for some new clothes while she waited for the news to break.

*

Chapter 9

Sam and Jeff were in Computer Lab, their fourth class of the day, when another teacher stuck her head in and asked their teacher to step outside for a minute. After the door closed, one of the boys got close to the door and listened in on their conversation.

"Holy crap! Mr. Lee was found dead this morning. His Facebook says he killed Bridgette..."

Everyone started searching the internet to see what could be found on Mr. Lee. The door opened and the boy barely got in his seat before the teacher walked back in the room. The whole class was talking and the room was buzzing about Mr. Lee.

"Well class, what has you so stirred up?"

"We just saw on the internet that Mr. Lee was found dead at home."

"I'm sorry to say, but it's true. I will be praying for him."

One boy said, "Good riddance, he was a pervert."

"Billy, that's uncalled for. You don't know that. Just because a bunch of kids thinks someone is bad, doesn't make them bad."

"Mrs. Stevens, Channel 5 News is reporting that they have received inside information that there were pictures of young girls and a suicide note on his Facebook account. They indicate that he may be responsible for Bridgette's disappearance."

"Michael, let me see what you have up on your computer. Bridgette's grandparents took her to live with them. Oh, this is bad. Real bad."

The news gave more detail as the day wore on and by the time Grumpy picked them up from school, most of the story was out in the open.

Sam and Kathy were talking with Jeff when Grumpy drove up. Their plan to use the evidence against Ms. Tapp was falling apart with the explosion wiping out the evidence and Mr. Lee claiming that he abducted Bridgette.

"Sam did any of you have Mr. Lee for any classes?"

Kathy and I haven't, he was a Chemistry and Physics teacher. Jeff did."

"Yes, I have had him for several classes. I have him now for Advanced Physics. I guess had him is more correct. He was an excellent teacher. He was weird around the girls though. He always stared at them and made them feel uncomfortable."

"Dad, I don't think he had anything to do with Bridgette's disappearance. I know it's Ms. Tapp.

"How do you know it's Ms. Tapp?"

"Excellent detective work. Let's discuss this when we get home please. I need your advice on this case."

"Are Kathy and Jeff working on this case?"

"Mr. Jones, we all are working on finding Bridgette. We didn't research Collins as you requested, but we found connections with him while researching Tapp."

"Well let's get GW and go over your findings after we sample the chocolate chip cookies that Martha and Mom made today."

The rest of the way home Sam tried to figure out how she would tell Grumpy how they got their evidence without lying. She was new to the religion thing, but was sure that lying was just about as bad as entering a home without permission. She wondered if God was ok with them picking locks and sneaking into houses if it saved a young girl's life.

They walked into the kitchen and the smell of fresh baked chocolate chip cookies filled the air. Mary poured a glass of milk for everyone and sat down at the kitchen table to enjoy the cookies and discuss their day. Sammy was begging bits of cookie from everyone and trying to be cute so he would get more crumbs.

"Sam, now can you fill us in on your brilliant detective work?"

"Yes, but we'll have to go to a monitor to see the evidence."

She proceeded to tell them the parts of the investigation leading up to entering the house.

GW said, "Too bad the house was blown to pieces before we could get in and look for evidence."

He thought for a second and said, "You didn't break into her house? Did you?"

Kathy spoke first, "Gramps, we knew that she was involved with the dead girls and Bridgette's kidnapping so we had to get the evidence. We didn't break in. We picked her back door's lock."

Sam spoke up, "Before you pass judgment, please look at these pictures."

Jeff hooked her phone up to Grumpy's big screen TV, there were the pictures from the basement, copies of all of the bank records and the list of girls ordered and filled. They saw the basement had been set up to hold prisoners and the names scratched in to the walls.

If these were obtained legally, they would be admissible and would make a good case against Ms. Tapp. If we give them to the law, they will want to know how we got them. Then your three are in deep dodo with the law. You are minors and won't go to jail, but Sam you could be taken from the Jones and you two would probably be kicked out of school."

Mary reacted by starting to cry and Grumpy was doing good just to control himself.

"Sam, we know that you had a rough upbringing, but all of you know that breaking into someone's home is a sin and against the law. Jeff, I can't punish you and won't tell your parents, but you need to leave here knowing that this can never happen again. Go home now."

"Dad, I'm so sorry. We just knew that we had to save Bridgette before they killed her or sold her to some pervert. I will never do anything stupid like that again."

GW said, Kathy, go to your room. We will talk later."

Mary said, "Sam, go to your room."

GW and Grumpy went out to the garage to work on Grumpy's truck. They worked for about an hour before anyone spoke.

"Grumpy, how can we be mad at them when you know darn well that we would have done the same thing to save a friend? We need to figure out how to get the police to sift through the rubble and find this evidence if it wasn't blown up."

"Grumpy started laughing and said, "I know. I would have done the same thing if I thought I had a chance to save a friend. Can you tip off the police?"

"I'll try. I think an anonymous call will work. I just have to find a pay phone where they can't trace the call back to me."

GW also told Grumpy about the missing person's flier and both agreed to chip in a thousand bucks towards the reward for information. GW told Kathy later that night.

"Hello Jeff. I'm sorry that we drug you into this freaking mess. I miss you. I didn't mean to hurt you or Kathy."

"Sam, I miss you too. You didn't make me go in that house. I want to find Bridgette just as much as you do. We can't stop just because of this setback. We learn from our mistakes, roll with the punches and come out stronger. Let's spend the evening coming up with a better plan. I'm going to do a little checking and maybe I have something later tonight. Good night."

"Sam, you told him that you miss him."

"So, he is a good friend. What is the big deal? I'd miss you too. Not a lot, but I'd miss you."

"Sam has a boyfriend."

"Okay, enough of that brains of a toad girl. Let's concentrate on finding Bridgette and making those who kidnapped her pay for their sins."

Sammy just lay on the bed listening to them fuss at each other. His head looked like he was watching a tennis match with his head going from Kathy to Sam and back. He tried his best to get them to play and he couldn't get them interested. He was happy to be with his girl, but sensed that she was still sad about this girl named Bridgette. He wanted his girl happy again.

The morning news had even more detail, which linked Mr. Lee with Bridgette's disappearance and was the topic of breakfast that morning.

Sam gave grace, "Lord thank you for your blessings to us and thanks for the friends around this table. Please watch over Bridgette and protect us from evil. Please forgive Mr. Lee for any sins and help us find his killer. Amen."

Grumpy spoke, "Have you girls thought about an appropriate punishment?"

Sam looked up and grinned as she said, "Well perhaps we should be like the Catholics."

"And what do you mean by that?"

"Make us say 10 Hail Marys and 10 Lord's Prayers."

Grumpy quickly replied, "I don't think that was funny."

The others at the table were laughing aloud.

GW added, "Grumpy, let's give them exactly what Sam asked for with a slight twist. They can write the Ten Commandments a hundred time each and underline the part about honoring thy father and mother."

"I like that."

The topic turned to the Lee suicide and the table erupted in opinions.

Sam said, "I think he was killed by Ms. Tapp to cover up her involvement with Bridgette's kidnapping.

Kathy agreed.

Mary added, "I find it hard to believe that Bridgette told Ms. Tapp about the abuse by her step father; Ms. Tapp doesn't report the abuse and Mr. Lee ends up being a child abductor who commits suicide. That's just too complicated for me. The least complicated answer is usually the correct answer."

"Let's start posting the fliers. Nana, can you and Mary have them printed up so we can start posting them?"

"Bill, please have them printed. Martha and I will pick them up and start by posting them in Louisville. I planned to go into town and do some shopping so we might as well post a few hundred fliers while we are there. We can go to Lexington and Elizabethtown also. The girls can post them in Newton and the surrounding small towns with Jeff as their chauffer."

Everyone agreed and Grumpy took the girls to school where Kathy and Sam posted several that she had printed last night. They hit all of the hallways and gathering places for the students.

It didn't take long for Kathy and Sam to be called to the principal's office.

"Girls have you seen these documents?"

"Yes."

"Did you post these documents?"

"Yes."

"Do you know that you have to have permission to post documents?"

"Yes, but everyone post things all of the time without getting permission. At least our postings are for a good cause and not just another dance or cookie sale."

"Look girls, I'm not here to persecute you, but rather to understand why you are posting these. The police are working on this case and shouldn't you stay out of their way."

Sam spoke up, "Sir, no disrespect intended, but the police are supposed to be working on who attacked our family, who killed all of those girls, who killed the two cops and who abducted Kathy's parents. Have they solved any of those crimes?"

The principal looked at the girls and said, "Post as many as you want to with my blessing. I'll take some home with me and post them all over Versailles. I'll make copies and have the teachers and staff that live in other cities do the same. If you'll make me an electronic copy on this thumb drive, I'll send it to every school in the state and ask them to post it in their towns. Good job ladies."

They both thanked him and went back to class. Over the next two days, the pictures were posted in just about every city and county in the state.

Ms. Tapp came to school for half a day and had meetings with the police and her insurance company in the afternoon. She saw one of the postings with Bridgette's picture and asked one of the students who had put up the posting. The student told her that Sam Smith had put them up all over the school and around town. She went to her office and had the secretary call Sam to her office.

"Samantha Smith you know that you are not to post anything without administrative approval. This is uncalled for since Bridgette was taken in by her grandparents."

"Mam, Bridgette was not taken in by her grandparent and is actually missing. The police are putting an Amber alert out for her today thanks to our efforts."

"You are in deep trouble and will be punished...."

The principal walked into the office and said, "Ms. Tapp, Samantha has my permission to post the fliers and I have personally sent copies to every school in the state. I have talked with the police and if not for Samantha and Kathy, no one would be looking for this poor girl. Someone murdered her parents and staged it to look like a suicide and again thanks to these two girls there is a murder investigation going on."

"Barry, I'm sorry. I didn't know that they had permission."

"We'll discuss this later. Sam, I'm sorry for the confusion and you can go back to class."

126

"Sir, Mr. Lee's death should also be investigated. It makes no sense and I believe the person who kidnapped Bridgette works for the same person who killed and kidnapped all of the girls at that cabin. I'm afraid that Bridgette has already been sold as a sex slave in a foreign country."

"Samantha, you have an over active imagination and ....."

"Ms. Tapp, Samantha and Kathy have been the only ones who figured out that Bridgette had been kidnapped and you forget that Samantha and her dad are the ones who broke the dead girl's case a few weeks ago. Samantha, have you gone to the police about Mr. Lee yet?

"No sir, we are doing some research and will meet with them this afternoon after school. Thanks for your support."

Sam left and went back to her class.

"Dot, I know that you are under stress, but you were out of line with Samantha and I want you to apologize to her tomorrow. That girl has a lot of untapped ability and I'd hate to have her after me for a crime. I'm going to encourage her to pursue a career in law enforcement."

Ms. Tapp was fuming on the inside as she left the principal's office. She thought, *"That brat is close to stumbling on everything that I've worked so hard to bury. If I don't stop her, I'll be dead or in jail. The Saudis won't want me in jail and talking to the police. I have to shut her up. Too bad I didn't run her ass down the other day. Now I have to meet with the police and get the third degree about my house."*

Sam told Kathy and Jeff about the run in with Ms. Tapp and the principal stepping in and supporting Sam and her efforts.

"Sam, she has to know that we are after her. You put it all out there under her nose."

"We have to be careful, she has possibly killed two people now and a couple of more won't bother her.

"She has already tried to kill Jeff and me the other day. Jeff, she has a blue Volvo with the Obama/Biden sticker. The same car tried to run us down. So, what's our plan? GW is anonymously sending clues to the evidence, but the explosion may have ruined all of it. We have to think that only we are going to solve Bridgette's kidnapping and prove Ms. Tapp did it."

Kathy replied, "I'll bet she killed Mr. Lee to get the police off her tail."

Ms. Tapp sat in the police station for almost an hour before someone came to get her.

"Hello, Ms. Tapp. I'm Detective Heath. Follow me and we'll sit down and discuss your house."

They walked down the hall and he led her into a windowless room with a large mirror on one wall. She had seen interrogation rooms before on TV. She wondered if they knew anything. There was a man already sitting in the room.

"Ms. Tapp, please meet Detective Black. He is working on the Bridgette Payne case. We think that your house blowing up, Bridgette's disappearance and Mr. Lee's death may all be connected. Black and I have been assigned to your case."

"Well I'm glad to assist in any way possible, but I don't think that I know anything helpful."

"Ms. Tapp this is a small town and we haven't had any serious crime here in over ten years. Oh, we get a few burglaries and a car theft every now and then when thugs from Louisville decide that we are easy picking, but we don't get murders and kidnappings. We have the Collin's case, the Cole's disappearance, Mr. Lee's suspicious death, the attacks on the Jones' family and two dead or missing police officers. Someone knows how or if they are all linked. Why would Mr. Lee blow your house up?"

"You think he blew my house up?"

"It's possible. Was he mad at you?"

"Yes he was, but that was over a year ago. Remember this department was investigating him for being a peeping tom. I helped the police with some background information and he confronted me about helping the police. I told him that if he was innocent, he didn't have anything to worry about."

"The principal told us that Lee told you that the Payne girl's parents had taken her to live with them in Idaho. Is this true? Did anyone witness this conversation?"

"Yes, he told me about the grandparents taking her to Idaho to live. I passed it on to the admin department. He came to my office and I don't remember anyone being in the room. Why do you think he may have blown up my house? He could

129

have killed me. Was he afraid that I could connect him with the girl's disappearance?"

"He would have known that you were in school. If he wanted to kill you, he would have set the explosives to go off at night. Is there anyone else that has a grudge with you? A teacher or a student?"

"No, not that I know of."

"What about your personal life? An abusive ex-boyfriend or husband?

"No, I never married and parted amicably with my last boyfriend. He thought I was too boring for him. A high school vice principal's life isn't very exciting and I just like to read and garden."

"Did any other children report being abused by parents or teachers?"

"No, there haven't been any recent cases reported. I did hear that the Smith girl was abused by her mom's boyfriend and may be pregnant by him."

"Darn, we forgot about that one. We'll check into that one also. You see Ms. Tapp, I don't believe in coincidence. We have no killings for a long time and suddenly we have people kidnapped, killed and houses blown up. There has to be a connection. Someone or something connects all of these events. I might be wrong, but I think I'm right."

He saw Ms. Tapp's face turn slightly red and her breath quicken as he questioned her. He also noticed that she wouldn't look him in the eyes."

"I'm glad to help in any way that I can, but that's all that I know."

"Have you heard back from the arson team from the KSP?"

"No, I hadn't thought about that. I guess we need their findings before my insurance can pay for rebuilding my house."

"Thanks for coming in today."

She was sweating, her face flushed and her heart racing as she walked to her car. She had never been so afraid in her life before. Even breaking into Lee's house and killing him was thrilling and she stayed calm even as he drew his last breath. Gary and these kids had to go. If Gary talked or the kids kept the police stirred up, she could go to the electric chair.

She knew that she had to kill all of them and then disappear. She would fake her death after eliminating the others.

*

Chapter 10

Grumpy and GW sealed the printouts of the pictures in a manila envelope and placed the correct number of stamps on the package. Grumpy dropped it in the mailbox and removed his gloves.

"Let's go eat and make the phone before heading home."

"Sounds good. Where do you want to eat?"

"Owensboro has some pretty good Bar B Q places, let's try one. They drove up Fredericka, turned down a side street and parked in front of Old Hickory Bar B Q. The placed smelled so good Grumpy fell in love at first smell. He ordered the brisket and GW ordered the pulled pork. The meals were excellent and the sweat tea was the best GW had ever had.

"Grumpy, you know that the police are going to go after Ms. Tapp and who ever she is working with. We could have another situation like you had with Collins. We need to be prepared."

"GW, what do you think about pulling the kids out of school and taking a two week vacation far away from here. We can get their teachers to give us their assignments and fax their homework back to the school. I don't want to go through this again."

"Good idea, but what about Jeff?"

"We'll take him along. He is as deep in this as we are. I like him and want to nurture his relationship with Sam. He really cares for her. A pregnant teen age girl probably has few chances at finding a boy mature enough to accept the baby and how independent Sam is."

"When do you adopt her?"

"Thanks for reminding me. I need to check with my lawyer and Greg Hope the Director of CHCS to see where we stand. We should be signing the papers in about a month."

"That was the best Bar B Q that I have ever had. I'm going to buy some to take home."

"Ok, I'm going to phone home and I wait in the truck."

He called Mary and received an update on her day.

"Bill, Detective Black dropped by today and asked me all kinds of questions about everything from Sam's abduction and the cabin explosion to our involvement with the Payne girl's disappearance. I told him everything that I knew except for what you asked me to hold back. He didn't know to ask about those items so I didn't have to lie to him. He did ask if I was afraid that someone might hurt us for digging into these crimes."

"Thanks for the update. What did you tell him about being afraid? I told him that I shot Jack Jr. and those biker gang thugs and would shoot anyone else trying to hurt my family."

"What did he say about that?"

"He said that he would never make me mad, excused himself and left."

"He thinks we know more than we are telling him. I don't think he thinks we have committed any crimes, but he wants more info. We sent the package and it should keep him busy."

A couple of days later Detective Black was at his desk when a clerk dropped a thick envelop on his desk. He put on a pair of latex gloves and opened the envelope. Inside he found a typed note. It read, *"Detective Black, these pictures are from Dorthea Tapp's house and basement before the explosion. The evidence suggests that she not only kidnapped the Payne girl, but also may have kidnapped many more. Three Middle Eastern men broke into her house and one called Dameer placed the explosive that destroyed the house. I believe they are Saudi Nationals. That's all I know; I can't do all of your work for you."*

Black picked up the phone, called the arson investigator and asked him to bring his team back to the house for another search. He explained the tip and the guy was eager to perform another search on the house. He called the FBI and asked them to look for the Saudis.

Three hours later, digging through debris, they found several notebooks burned on the outside, with the inner pages only burned on the edges. Black found the books that matched the photos. One of the arson investigators waived at him from what was left of the basement and showed him the chain bolted to the steel pole, the burnt mattress and another was taking pictures of the wall. Black could see that the mattress had been against the wall so he hoped that the names scratched into the paint would still be legible.

The investigator lifted the camera to Black and he looked at the screen. There were at least five legible names and Bridgette Payne's name was one of them. Bingo, we got her sorry ass.

"Hello Chief, this is Black, we've got her by the short hair. The arson squad and I found where people have been chained to a pole, a mattress, incriminating logbooks and Bridgette Payne's name scratched into a wall by the mattress. I need a warrant for Tapp's arrest."

"You know that she will just lawyer up on us. Get it done; we don't need her around our kids."

Ms. Tapp wanted to look at what was left of her former house as she drove over to her insurance agent. She turned onto her block and saw several police cars and police officers searching the rubble. She turned around, parked on a side street, walked up the alley to the house next to hers and hid behind the neighbor's wooden fence. She heard bits and pieces of the conversation. When she heard, *Logbooks, chain and names scratched,*" she took off back to her car. She knew that she had to hide until she figured out what to do. She also knew that she had to tie up loose ends or they would haunt her forever.

She couldn't go back to the hotel so she drove to the outskirts of town and parked on a dirt road. She needed to ditch her car and find a place to stay. Then it came to her Phil had never been reported missing. She would go to his house. She pulled off the dirt road into some bushes and weeds and took a nap until later that evening.

She had been to Phil's house a couple of times and spent the night once after too much wine. She woke up in bed with Phil the next morning not remembering a thing about the night. She drove into his driveway and saw his Lexus sitting next to the house. She broke the back passenger's side window, got in the car and used the remote to open the garage door. She parked the Volvo in the garage and went cautiously into the house. It was neat and looked like he had just left. She picked the newspapers off the porch and got the mail from the mailbox. She then checked the refrigerator and pantry to see what she could find and made a meal of fried pork chops with a salad.

She searched his house and found a .38 revolver and a tin lockbox with a couple thousand dollars. She could drive Phil's car for a couple of day, but needed more money to head to California. She went back into the garage and retrieved her Bugout Bag from the trunk. There were her fake ID's, a 9 mm Glock, a change of clothes and $5,000 in twenties and hundred dollar bills. She just had to find that pesky Sam Smith, kill her and hit the road. She knew that she didn't have time to kill all of them, but maybe she would get lucky and find them all together.

She called her friend Gary and invited him to Phil's house to discuss their first order for girls. She knew that he would come if she dangled the new business. She would shoot him and then go kill the girl tonight. Gary was eager to discuss the new business and would be there at 9:00 sharp.

Her asthma acted up and her medicine was at the hotel. She found a ball cap, sunglasses and a jacket to disguise herself. She drove the Lexus to the nearest gas station, filled up and bought some medicine.

*

Chapter 11

It was finally the big day for Sam and Jeff's date. Grumpy gave Jeff the keys to the Mustang and told him to take the car to his house and clean it up for their date. Jeff was so glad that the ordeal with Bridgette and Ms. Tapp was over. The police were searching for Ms. Tapp though they were speculating that she had fled to California. Sam's mind was off the case and she agreed to go on a date with Jeff. He was taking her to dinner and a movie. There was a new Post-Apocalyptic movie, Hell in the Homeland, playing at the Newton Theater. They both were into Science Fiction and were eager to see it. Jeff washed, waxed and cleaned the interior of the Mustang, just as if were his. He was actually a little jealous of Sam for having such a beautiful car. Her birthday was next week and Grumpy and Mary had a party planned and were giving it to her then.

Jeff went into the house to get ready and his dad stopped him to say, "Son, that's a nice car and you need to be careful not to wreck it tonight. Mr. Jones must like and trust you, to let you borrow it for a date with Sam."

"Dad, Mr. Jones is giving the car to Sam for her birthday next week. He says that I can drive it on our dates."

"Son, how serious are you about this girl?"

"Dad, I've liked Sam since we were little kids. You know me; I've always been too bashful to tell her that I liked her. I know that Mom and you have reservations about me dating a pregnant girl, but I like her and would be dating her if she wasn't pregnant."

"Son, a young pregnant girl needs a husband to provide and care for her. We want you to go to college. Your mom and I barely got out of high school and while we aren't dirt poor we want better for you."

"Dad, I'm going to college one way or the other. I'm sure that I will get offers of scholarships to several good schools. Don't worry about that."

Jeff went to his room and started getting ready for his first date.

Sammy jumped in her lap staring at her belly when he started barking. He saw her belly move again and Sammy lay on her belly and followed the movement.

"Kathy, the baby is playing with Sammy."

"Let me see? Hey, you'd better stop fooling around and get ready. You can wear some of my jewelry if you want to. My

139

tennis bracelet and diamond pendent will go nicely with your blouse. Do you even have a purse?"

"Of course I do. I just choose to use my backpack at school and everyday use. Can you help me with my hair? It's kinda flat and freaking me out. Can you curl it for me?"

"I think that would be beautiful on you. Why are you so nervous? You still say that you don't like Jeff."

"I guess that I do like him and I don't want him disappointed when he picks me up tonight."

"Sister, has your mom given you the sex talk? You don't need to lose your virginity tonight. Kissing is ok, but no petting or taking your clothes off."

"Sam shook her fist at Kathy and twirled her body around several times and said, "Yes, I can see where a man would want my fat butt. I look like an alien is growing inside me and is waiting to jump out and kill kids in a cabin on a lake. He should be running the other way."

She plopped down on the bed lying on her back beside Sammy, who cuddled up against her and barked every time the baby kicked him.

"See, I look like a beached whale."

"Well love is strange."

Sam threw a pillow at Kathy and went to the bathroom for her shower. Sam should have been thinking about Jeff and her date that night, but could only think about putting Ms. Tapp in jail and finding Kathy's parents.

Sam heard the Mustang pull into the driveway. It had a deep throaty sound that is distinctive to big displacement high-powered engines. Jeff knocked on the door and Mary let him in. He gave her some flowers and talked with her and Grumpy until Sam came down the steps.

He saw her, had a big goofy grin on his face and said, "Sam, you are beautiful."

He was a gentleman; he opened her door and helped her get in the Mustang. They drove off and were out of sight in a minute. Grumpy was impressed that Jeff drove the Mustang slower than expected and shifted it very smoothly.

"Thanks for saying that I am beautiful in front of Mom and Dad; that meant a lot to me."

"I didn't just say it Sam. I meant it."

The radio was on and just as Jeff reached to turn it off a news bulletin was broadcasted. They heard that the police were searching for Ms. Dorthea Tapp, the vice principal at the local high school. She was wanted in connection to the disappearance of Bridgette Payne.

"Yeah, they finally are going to put Ms. Tapp away. Jeff we did it. She will be arrested and tried for her crimes."

"I am glad that this is about over. I want us to have a more normal life."

"Jeff, I love the challenge and excitement. I will miss all of the investigation and tracking down the bad guys. I'm thinking about becoming a detective."

"I want to be an IT developer and lead a boring life. I guess dating you will be all the excitement that I can stand."

She squeezed his hand and said, "I know that you love the excitement also. Don't kid me."

The movie was great and Jeff held her hand for the whole time. She saw couples sitting on the back row hugging and kissing and thought, *"Maybe we can do that later after the baby was born."*

She was starting to feel a strong attachment to Jeff and she knew that he cared for her. That dating thing might be good after all.

After the movie, Jeff took her to a Chinese restaurant and they enjoyed talking to each other about each other and not about who shot whom. Jeff was happy that they got away from the investigation and he could just enjoy Sam's company. They talked for half an hour after Jeff had paid the bill. They were sitting by the front window and saw a couple from school walking past the window. They both waived, but then something caught Sam's attention across the street at the gas station.

"Jeff, look at that that woman with the ball cap and sunglasses. Why the sunglasses after dark? Hey, that's Ms. Tapp. Come on. We have to follow her."

She jumped up and headed out to the car with Jeff in tow.

"Sam, we're not sure that it is even her."

"I know, but I think it's her and we will follow her to make sure before we call the police. Fire the Mustang up and don't lose her."

The Lexus was pulling out of sight as they pulled out of the parking lot. Jeff pushed the pedal down and the Lexus taillights were back in view. The car passed under a street light and they could see that it was the same Lexus. They followed from a distance until the car turned into a subdivision and Jeff

142

backed off a bit. They saw it turn into a driveway and watched as the woman got out and went in a side door by the garage.

"Jeff we have to get closer so we can ID her. I need to peep through a window."

"Sam, you can get shot. Someone might think that you are a peeping Tom."

She got out, walked across the street and walked across the backyards until she saw a dog following her. It didn't bark and walked straight to her.

"Sammy?"

The little dog ran up and jumped in her arms.

"Jeff, how did Sammy get in the car? He's been chaperoning us all along. Sammy be, quiet so we can spy on Ms. Tapp. Jeff, take him back to the car and make sure he can't get out."

Sammy heard the name and growled.

She snuck down the back yards until she were on the side of the house. Sam looked in and saw Ms. Tapp taking her jacket off and taking some type of medicine. Jeff joined her a few minutes later.

She turned to Jeff and said, "Jeff, we need to call the police. "

Before she could turn, "Jeff said, "We have company."

There was a tall guy in the shadows with a gun pressed into Jeff's side.

"I heard you mention Ms. Tapp. Why are two snot nosed kids stalking her?"

"Neither answered so he said, "Move we are going to introduce you to Dot."

He knocked on the door and saw the blinds move, then the door opened.

"Gary, where did you find these two trouble makers?"

She was ecstatic. Three out of five people who had to die were right in front of her. She had planned to kill Gary and then go after the two girls, but as long as Sam was taken out, she would be happy.

"They were sneaking around outside this house. They must have followed you. What do you want to do with them? We could sell him to the Saudis. They also like cute boys just like him, but a pregnant girl is worthless to them."

"Search them and destroy their phones. Tie them up and put them on the couch. We will determine what to do with them after I question them."

Gary tore the cords off two of the window blinds and bound their hands behind them. Jeff immediately started trying to get free himself from the bindings, but was making little progress. He noticed that Sam was working on hers also when no one was looking.

"Why have you been investigating me? I am innocent and yet you have the police after me. What did I ever do to Kathy and you?"

"Will you let us go if we tell you and promise not to bother you again? Please don't hurt Sam and her baby."

"Is the baby yours?"

"No, but I would be proud to be the father."

"Oh, such a gentleman. I guess the good news for you is that you two will die together with the baby."

She knew that she had to get rid of Gary first so she could use his gun with his fingerprints to kill these two.

"Gary, be a dear and go to the Lexus and get my bag out of the back seat."

"Ok, but we need to handle these two quickly and then we probably want to burn this house down around them."

Gary started out the door and got as far as opening the door when Tapp said, "Gary, close the door."

He turned to see what was going on and she shot him twice. He stood there and looked at her as if to say, *Why me?*"

"Sorry Gary, but you are the only one who could tie me directly to Lee's death and the slave trade."

Gary fell to his knees, yet still did not fall to the floor Ms. Tapp walked over and pushed him until he fell. She pulled a pair of gloves out of a bag on the floor and put them on.

"You still didn't answer my question. Why did you try so hard to prove me guilty?

*

Chapter 12

Sammy was going berserk in the Mustang. He barked and clawed at the window until a woman out for a run stopped and saw him.

"Poor boy, someone left you in this car. You are such a pretty Shih Tzu. Come on out."

She opened the door; Sammy took off across the street and barked at the side door of the house two houses down. She saw lights on and thought that she would give the owner a piece of her mind. She ran over to the door that the dog was barking at and knocked on the door. When no one answered, she beat on the door until it opened.

"Look you have no business locking that poor dog..."

She shut up abruptly when she saw the gun in her face. Ms. Tapp pulled her into the room, shoved her to the floor and kicked her in the side.

"Please stop and don't hurt me."

Ms. Tapp didn't see Sammy sneak in behind the woman. He ran over behind Jeff while Tapp was busy with the woman. He started biting at the cord

The woman saw the dead man and the puddle of blood and started crying and begging for her life.

"Please don't kill me; I have a husband and two kids. I have to be there for them."

Sammy had eaten through one cord and working on the other when Tapp said, "Lady, shut up and die like a woman instead of a sniveling baby."

The last cord broke just as she raised the gun. Jeff sprang to action, tackled her below the waist and knocked her to the ground. Sammy piled on and started biting her hand and arms. She grabbed the gun, hit Jeff on the head and knocked him out. Sammy kept attacking until she shot at him twice. He ran and hid.

Ms. Tapp was bleeding from the bites and a gash on her head from hitting it on the fireplace as she fell from being slammed to the floor. She was having trouble thinking and regaining her awareness of the situation.

Sam noticed and said, "Ms. Tapp, are you okay. You hit your head and you are losing a lot of blood. Untie me and I will help you."

Ms. Tapp started over to Sam, then slowed and looked around the room and slurred, "You are trying to trick me."

Sammy was sneaking down the hallway when suddenly the door slammed open and a woman ran in and knocked Ms. Tapp to the floor and took her gun.

"Who are you? Please untie me so I can take care of my boyfriend."

"I have business to take care of first. Ms. Tapp, sit on the couch beside Sam and put your hands behind you."

She took the cord that had been on Jeff and tied Tapp's hands behind her. She then untied Sam.

"I freed you, but don't try to stop me or I'll hurt you and I don't want to hurt a pregnant woman."

Sammy was licking Jeff's face and Sam picked his head up and placed it on her lap.

"Jeff, please wake up. I need you to take care of Sammy and me."

Jeff moaned and moved his head, then opened his eyes. Sam had to hold him down until he calmed down.

Jeff looked at the woman and said, "Bridgette, is that you?"

"Well Jeff, how did you recognize me?"

"I've been in school with you for 11 years. A little makeup and hair dye doesn't change how you look."

Sam punched him on the shoulder.

"What did I do?"

"Jeff, Sam must be your girlfriend. She'll tell you later what you did."

"Bridgette, call the police. We have been looking for you since you disappeared. We knew it was Ms. Tapp and now we have her. The police will make sure that she never hurts anyone again."

"Sorry Sam, but I have dreamed about meeting up with Ms. Tapp for weeks now and I won't turn her over to the police. You two get out of here and I'll make sure that she doesn't hurt anyone again. GO!"

Jeff struggled to get up with Sam's help and was still a bit groggy.

"Bridgette, I don't know you like Sam and Kathy, but do you really want to be a killer? Killing this wicked and depraved woman won't make you feel better and you will be looking over your shoulder for the rest of your life. That is until the law puts you in jail."

"Too late Jeff, I am a killer and I am specializing in eliminating filth like this as my new profession. Go now or watch her die."

Jeff reached into his pocket and whispered, "Bridgette, take this and use the information wisely. The account numbers and passwords are active. Everything but the account numbers and passwords went to the police. Act quickly."

The neighbor lady helped get him to the Mustang and ran to her house.

They left the house and Sam had to drive them away from the area. She stopped at the first gas station and called 911 for the police and an ambulance. Then she called Grumpy.

"Dad, Bridgette is alive and has probably killed Ms. Tapp by now. Jeff was hit in the head and I think he is okay, but I want a doctor to check on him. Can you meet us at the hospital and have someone get the Mustang? We are at the GasMart at the corner of Broad and Market Street. I called 911. I'll fill you in later."

149

"Sam, are you ok? Is Sammy with you?"

"I am fine and Sammy is with us."

"We are leaving now; Martha and GW will get the car and join us at the hospital."

"Dad, call Jeff's parents."

"I will. I love you Sam. We'll be right there."

The ambulance arrived and the EMTs checked Jeff and Sam out and loaded them into the ambulance. Sammy jumped in and rode to the hospital with them.

"Mam, you won't be able to take the dog in to the hospital."

"I know. My mom and dad will meet us there."

"Okay."

Grumpy and Mary arrived just ahead of the ambulance. Grumpy took Sammy while Mary stayed with Sam. Jeff's parents arrived a few minutes later and rushed to Jeff's side. GW arrived about 15 minutes later and took Sammy home.

One of the ER Nurse Practitioners checked Sam out and told them that she was in good health and the baby's heartbeat was strong. She wanted Sam to spend the night at the hospital so they could make sure that Sam and the baby were okay. The Doctor said that Jeff didn't have a concussion and sent him to have an x-ray performed to make sure. His parents came to see how Sam was doing.

His mom said, "Jeff should be ok; he doesn't have a concussion and they are performing the x-ray to make sure. You both are lucky that mad woman didn't kill you both."

"Mrs. Stone, do you mean Ms. Tapp? She was a very bad person and would have killed us the first time if Jeff hadn't tackled her and gave time for Bridgette to get there and free us. Ms. Tapp hit Jeff on the head when he tackled her. Sammy attacked her and kept her from shooting us until Bridgette knocked her down and took her gun."

Sam had just finished when she saw a uniformed officer and Detective Black enter the room and said, "Sam, I'm Detective Black and I've been working on the Payne and Lee cases. I'd like to hear what you have to say about last night."

Grumpy walked over to him, pulled him off to the side and asked him a couple of questions, "Is Tapp still alive and does Jeff and Sam need a lawyer?"

"Mr. Jones, I just want to hear what they know about Ms. Tapp attacking them and what they saw? Someone killed Ms. Tapp and a man in that house and we need to find out what Jeff and Sam know. We know they were there from Sam's call. We don't believe that Sam and Jeff committed any crimes and do believe they were victims.'

"Okay, go ahead."

Sam filled him in on everything from seeing Ms. Tapp at the gas station to Bridgette Payne saving their lives.

"Mr. Black, what happened to Ms. Tapp? Will she come after us again?"

"Honey, Ms. Tapp died last night and won't bother anyone anymore. If Bridgette contacts you, please tell her to call me."

He gave Grumpy his business card and told them that he like them to come to the police station to get their comments in writing.

He turned to leave and said, "Young lady when you grow up, think about going into law enforcement. You, your friends and family have done a good job solving several crimes, but you need to leave crime fighting to the pros, it can be dangerous.

Jeff and Sam found to be in good health, were released at noon. Grumpy took everyone to his favorite restaurant for lunch. They took the time to bring Jeff's parents up to speed on everything from Sam's kidnapping to Ms. Tapp.

Jeff's mom said, "Y'all certainly lead a dangerous life. I'm not sure I like Jeff being around so much violence."

"Ah, Mom, we didn't do anything dangerous. The bad guys just don't want the truth to come out."

"Jeff, what would have happened if Bridgette hadn't saved y'all at the last minute?"

"Sam or Sammy would have found a way. God is watching over us and wanted us to stop these crimes. I really believe that he is using Sam and Sammy to stop the abduction of these young girls."

Jeff's father chimed in, "Y'all tip toed around Jack Collins Sr. He has to be involved and has to be stopped or the girls will keep disappearing."

"Adam, that is true. We are steering the police towards him, but he has bought off too many politicians and police. We may not get him, but we will keep trying."

"What can we do to help?"

"I'm not sure at this point. We are only searching the internet and gathering information at this time. I promise to involve you when the time comes. Jeff has been a big help with the internet searches. If you don't mind we want to take him on vacation with us for several days down to Cumberland falls."

Grumpy took Sam off to the side and told her about the real missions and Sam was ok with the trip.

Jeff's mom said, "Jeff won't be sleeping in the same room with the girls, will he?

Mary quickly replied, "Heavens no. Those two are getting closer by the day and that would be a little too close. I'll watch over them."

Sam said, "It's not like we're going to do anything. Jeff is too much a gentleman and I'm a big hippo barely able to waddle. I don't see how anyone would want kids if they have to go through this."

Bridgette was very happy and relieved at the same time. She slept well that night and woke to a beautiful day. Ms. Tapp was history and she could now focus on her new life. She gathered her clothes from the previous night and intended to burn them in the fire pit in the back yard. She checked her pockets and found the memory stick that Jeff had placed in her hand. She burned the clothes to get rid of any blood spatter and then went back in the house to check out Jeff's gift.

She plugged it in to her computer and found the evidence against Ms. Tapp and a picture of a page with what looked like bank account numbers and passwords. The largest accounts were in the Grand Caymans the smallest were in local banks.

She spent the next several days starting over ten bank accounts with different banks including new ones in the Grand Caymans. She moved every cent several times from bank to bank until she had most of the money in two off shore accounts. She set up ongoing wire transfers of $3,000 to each of her bank accounts each month and marked the money as alimony. She placed $9,000 in her other backup accounts.

She was ready to start her new life as a crime fighter. In her mind robbing and eliminating dope dealers and sex traffickers was a good thing. She would do what the law couldn't do. She scheduled herself for IT and Criminology courses at KY Wesleyan and then sought out courses in self - defense and shooting. She didn't want luck to have any role in her efforts; she wanted to be the best.

She thought back to Jeff placing that memory stick in her hands and set up a fund to pay for his college at UL. As an afterthought, she did the same for Kathy and Sam. This helped her conscious and made it feel better to take that $1.5 million dollars from Ms. Tapp.

*

Chapter 13

"Gramps, do you think that you could teach me how to safely shoot guns? I know that I am only 16, but I don't want to be like my mom and forbid dad to have a gun. I want to be able to defend myself. This whole deal with Ms. Tapp scared me. Sam and Jeff could have been killed."

"Darling, do you want to be able to defend yourself or shoot guns?

"Both I think, now that you put it that way."

"I'll begin with an hour a day of hand to hand training the rest of this week and then we'll spend half a day on Sunday training hand to hand when Grumpy and I get back from the Collins cabin. I'll also buy you some mace and a whistle. Then later we can talk about gun training. "

"Gramps, Sam, Jeff and I want to go to the cabin with you. We had planned to bring it up tomorrow. The cabin is the one thing that ties all of the Collins men together and is the site of some of the murders. We don't think the cops performed a thorough investigation and want to take a look at the basement, sheds and search the woods and land around the cabin."

"Let me think about it and I want to make sure that it would be safe. We could use a larger search party."

GW received a call from the KSP stating the report was sent by e-mail to GW and a copy to Grumpy. While this surprised GW, he didn't expect to see anything new in the report. He printed off a couple of copies and took them to Grumpy out in the garage. Grumpy was in the war room reviewing the data that the kids had compiled.

"Grumpy, this is the report that we requested from the KSP. I doubt that we will see anything new in it."

They read the report and as expected, it backed up Lt. Needmore's verbal report.

"Someone just wanted to delay us until they can get ahead of us."

Grumpy looked up from the report and said, "Or eliminate us. Do you think that Ms. Tapp supplied girls to Collins?"

"Yes I do. Do you think that we are getting paranoid?"

"Not at all. Even if we are, a bit of precaution goes a long ways."

"You got that right."

"What do you think about taking the wives and kids to the cabin to help with the search?"

"I think that we can pack up and all drive to Cumberland Falls Friday night for the week end to fool anyone trying to follow us. Then get up before dawn and drive the 130 miles to the cabin. You and I will check out the cabin before we call the girls and Jeff to join us. We'll hide our vehicles in the woods a short ways from the cabin and keep on the lookout for visitors. I'll get some remote motion detectors from my friend and place them across the only road into the area and we will be warned at least 15 minutes warning."

"You said that there was only one way in and out."

Grumpy replied, "We'd have to hide until they leave. There were fifty cops and thirty cars and trucks all over the way in and around the cabin so no one would notice a few extra foot prints."

"Sounds like a plan. Let's decide on what gear and weapons to take."

"Does, Martha know how to handle a gun?"

"Yes, she has her CCW permit and carries a Para 9mm. She is a good shot and I don't think that she would get rattled if she had to shoot at a bad guy."

"Mary shot Jack Jr. and took two bullets in the fight. They weren't major wounds, but she is still in pain and limping from the wounds. Sam is a good shot and please keep this to yourself, but she shot four or five of the motorcycle gang by herself with my .45 Colt."

"That reminds me that Kathy wants to learn how to shoot. Normally I would like that, but I don't want to see her storming into Collins office blasting away one day."

"I think Kathy has a good head on her shoulders and you don't have to worry about that. Take it slow and keep after the self-defense training then see how you feel in a couple of months.

Grumpy picked Sam and Jeff up, took them home after school, and used the time to get an update on their investigation.

"Mr. Jones, we don't have anything new, just more of the same. Kathy found 23 more missing girls that fit the pattern. The one thing that struck us is that many of these girls are missing from foster homes and that made us think about how many girls were missing from orphanages back in the 50s and 60s before the current foster care system."

"Good thinking. I'll have my PI check on them since it will require going through archives in Frankfort."

"Thanks Dad. We have built a huge data base on missing girls and the scary part is that the amount of missing girls doesn't taper off the further we get from Louisville."

"Jeff, can you get into any national missing children data base and filter out all but the ones that fit the profile."

"We should have thought about that. Don't worry Sam, Kathy's and your work still had to be done, but this will give us a good idea how big a problem that this is. I'll also highlight every city where Collins has property or businesses."

"Dad, we want to go with you to the cabin this weekend. We think that we can find more evidence. Both Collins Jr. and Sr. could have hidden mementoes from the girls similar to the locks of hair that he showed you. Many pedophiles keep articles of clothing, toys or other items to obsess over later."

158

"I see that you have been reading up on the subject and thanks for your choice of words. I hate that a young lady has to read about pedophiles."

"Me too, but the more I know the more I know what to look for in solving this case."

"I'll discuss the trip to the cabin with GW and let you know our decision. I had already thought that we would take Martha and your mom with us to the cabin to help search. Jeff, check with your parents and see if you can go."

"I will, thanks for including me."

The week passed slowly as Jeff and the girls continued the internet search and completing the database on the missing girls. Grumpy made reservations at the Cumberland Falls Lodge and told everyone he met in town on his errands that they were all going to get away for the weekend. He told Sam to do the same thing at school. He figured that Collins would have someone keeping tabs on them and a little misdirection wouldn't hurt any.

Jeff's parents gave him permission to go on the short vacation with the Jones and were worried about his safety because of the ongoing investigation of Collins. Jeff's dad agreed that the search had to take place. He was just sorry that he couldn't go with them.

"Deke, the targets appear to be heading out on a short vacation with their families on Friday. I will have two cars following them. Jones mentioned that they were heading down to Cumberland Falls for the weekend. I'll keep you posted."

"Thanks for the update. Keep me posted."

This was good news, now they just had to get Jones and Cole in the same car and make it have an accident away from home without involving the girl.

"Jerry, have you ever been to Cumberland Falls? Our targets are taking a weekend vacation."

"Never been there. Good a road trip is just what we need. It will be difficult to catch the two men away from the girl, but nothing is impossible with a little cash. Add another chase car to make sure the tail isn't made. I'm heading down there now with my men to scout the area for dangerous roadways."

Deke laughed and replied, "Yeah, we need to report any of those and get them fixed before someone gets hurt."

Grumpy picked up Sam and Jeff at school as usual and took Jeff by his house to pick up his bag. They planned to leave immediately and get supper at the Falls. The rest were loaded up and ready to go when Grumpy pulled in to the driveway. Grumpy had Mary and all three of the kids in the van with GW and Martha following in the Jaguar. They drove straight to the lodge and arrived two and a half hours later.

Grumpy got out of the van and said, "I'll get the keys to our rooms while y'all stretch your legs."

He walked into the lodge office, checked in, got the keys to three rooms, returned to his group and gave GW his key. They had adjoining rooms with a door between the rooms.

"Sam, you will stay with Kathy and Jeff will sleep in our room. We both have two double beds so everyone should be comfortable. Let's meet at the Lodge Restaurant lobby in 20 minutes. I'm hungry."

They all took their bags in and were assembled in the lobby on time. They didn't notice the guy snooping around their cars while they were eating or the couple seated a couple of tables over in the restaurant.

The woman placed a GPS tracking device on both the van and the Jaguar while the man watched the targets in the restaurant. Then they got into a van parked three rooms down from Grumpy's that had a good view of the rooms and parking lot. They joined their comrades in the van and began to take turns watching the targets the rest of the night. The man sent Deke a text with an update.

Grumpy woke up at 4:00 am and dressed without turning on the lights. He woke Mary and Jeff and took them to the bathroom to make sure they knew the plans for the day. He was paranoid about someone trying to listen in on their plans.

Before he could get started she said, "You and GW will leave here and spend about an half hour back tracking and making sure that no one is following you. We will do the same when we leave. Then you will drive straight to the cabin. We will leave the Lodge one hour after you leave. You will stop and install the motion detectors where the last road splits off the main road and then again at 200 yards before the cabin. You will park in the woods and walk through the woods to the cabin. Once you have made sure it's safe you will call us and then we can join you. If you don't call, we are not to follow you and are to call the police. Oh, keep your guns handy."

"Good, other than sounding like a robot, you have it down pat. I love you and don't do anything that will cause you or Sam to get hurt. Bye."

He kissed her and slid out the door to see GW sitting in the Jag ready to leave. He got in and GW pulled out of the parking lot heading west, away from the cabin for a couple of miles and turned into a parking lot and waited to see if any cars were behind them while Grumpy scanned the car for tracking devices which he didn't find any. They pulled out and drove around the area until they were certain that no one was following them.

"Where the hell are those two going at this hour? Wait about thirty minutes and send the signal to turn on the tracking device. That gives them time to check for tails and to sweep the car for tracking devices."

He sent a text to Deke, stating that the two targets were on the move without the girl. The text was received by Dekes' phone and the alert went off waking Deke. He read it and replied, *"Accidents happen. Take all resources to make sure."*

All three vehicles pulled out of the Lodge parking lot and began following the Jag via the GPS signal.

Mary knocked on the door between the rooms.

Martha opened the door and said, "I don't want to be a detective if they have to get up this early."

"You got that right girl. Let's be in the van in thirty minutes. I'm leaving a little early because I'm stopping for some coffee and a biscuit to eat on the road."

"Yeah"

Jeff was dressed quickly and calmly waited on the women to get ready.

"Mary said, "Sorry boy, but four women take a little longer than a man to get ready. Just as she spoke, Sam and Sammy came into the room. Sam had a blue shorts and a white T-shirt with a UK ball cap on her head.

"Well some women have to fix their hair."

Sammy jumped in Jeff's lap and lay still waiting on the others to get ready.

"Jeff, my dog has taken to you. I think I could be jealous if I weren't hungry."

"Here nibble on this cookie until we get breakfast."

Sammy jumped up and begged for a cookie until Jeff gave in and shared.

"Oh crap, I forgot Sammy's dog food. He'll have to eat human food for two days. Poor dog."

Martha looked in the room and said, "Hey, we're ready. Let's go."

"Just a minute, everyone check to make sure that you have your bugout bags. Martha do you have your pistol? Sam, here is a bag with a .45 Colt and a hundred rounds. Don't open it unless we are under fire."

"Mary, I have mine and I just placed the shotguns in the car."

"Jeff, place a shotgun near you just in case the stuff hits the fan."

"Thanks, I will only use it if forced to."

"Now I'll lead us in a prayer."

They all bowed their heads and Mary prayed, "Lord, we go in peace on a mission to find who is responsible for these atrocities and ask you to watch over us today. Amen."

They loaded into the van and Mary drove out of the parking lot and used the same routine that Grumpy used see if anyone was following. While there were more cars an hour later, none appeared to be following them. Mary then headed to the cabin driving for a few minutes before finding a place open to get some coffee and breakfast.

Sam went to the restroom while they ordered and went back to the van to wait. As she sat down, she saw a black thing that looked like a short flat baseball bat between the driver and passenger's seats. She placed it on her mom's seat so she would remember to ask about it. They all came back to the van and Jeff gave Sam her sausage biscuits and milk and got in his seat.

Mary sat down and said, "What am I sitting on? Oh darn, I forgot to sweep the van for tracking devices. She got out of the van and started walking around it holding the device close to the side. Suddenly Sammy started barking to get out.

Sam said, "Let him out now, that sausage may have disagreed with his stomach. We don't need dog poop in the van. Sammy jumped out just as Mary had cleared the van and was ready to get back in. He started barking again, went under the van and barked at something under the van.

Mary asked, "Jeff would you be a sweetheart and look under the van to see what he is barking at."

Jeff got down on his knees and looked under the van. He reached under and his hand came back empty. He looked for a few minutes and didn't see anything. Sammy went back under the car and found a plastic device with a five-inch wire sticking out of it. Sammy was chewing on it when Jeff grabbed for him so they could leave and knocked the device out of his mouth.

They drove on towards the cabin, not knowing that Sammy had gotten rid of the tracking device.

"Deke, I hate to disturb you this early, but we just figured out that they are headed to that cabin you mentioned in the briefing. They are about 20 minutes from the cabin and we are another 20 minutes behind them. Any instructions?

Deke knew the answer to his next question before he opened his mouth, "You were supposed to maintain visual contact with the target at all times. How are you tracking their car?"

"Deke, we had to use a tracking devise. This place is out in the sticks and it would have been too easy for them to spot us if we followed them by sight. Don't worry we will remove the tracking devices after the issue is resolved."

"Devices?"

"Yes, we placed one on both vehicles. The women and boy stayed at the Lodge so we didn't turn the tracking device on."

"Turn it on and make damn sure that they are not following you."

He quickly sent the signal to turn the device on and saw the van stopped on the side of the road a few miles from the Lodge. He reported this back to Deke.

"Good, you have a green light with the girl out of the way. Make sure that the van doesn't double back and head to the cabin."

"We will Boss."

"GW, turn right at the next road. We are only about 15 miles from the cabin. I need to place the motion detector at the next turn and it's just up there on the left. Turn left and stop."

Grumpy got out of the car and placed the motion detectors on both sides of the road. It was set to detect only large objects and would send a radio signal to a small receiver in his pocket when a car passed by.

They drove on to the Cabin and parked just short of the driveway in some weeds and brush. They cut some brush and covered the backend of the Jag and where the Jag went into the woods. Mary had been instructed to do the same.

They watched the area around the hole where the cabin had been and didn't see any movement. Grumpy signaled that he would circle around the back of the remains of the cabin. Grumpy slowly walked around to the back while keeping an eye out for trip wires and motion detectors. He didn't find any. He arrived at the back of what was left of the cabin and waved GW to come join him.

"The coast is clear; I'll call Mary and tell them to come on to the cabin."

He tried, but couldn't get a connection so he sent a text. He knew that a text would go through when they got cell reception.

"Let's look around the sheds first while we wait on the others to arrive."

"Good idea, I'll take the big one behind the cabin and you take that one to the left. Keep your eyes and ears open until we can post a watch. Look for hidden doors and hiding places."

Grumpy walked into the same shed that Jack had taken him into to get the shovel to dig his own grave. A shutter ran through him as he remembered seeing the locks of hair from many girls hanging on the wall. They were gone now and setting in a CSI lab in Frankfort. He saw that the shed was nearly empty since the police had taken all of the tools to check for blood. He pried on boards and pushed on walls for several minutes when he heard GW yell for him. He moved over to where GW was searching.

GW was holding a trap door open and said, "The bastards have a hidden room under this shed. Look at the foam block of insulation. They didn't want anyone to hear what was going on down there. Hold it up and I'll go down the steps and see what's down there."

He turned his flashlight on and carefully went down the steps.

"Damn, something's dead down here the odor is terrible. Holy crap, there are two decaying bodies and both are small women or girls. I'm taking some pictures and getting back to the surface."

Grumpy saw the flashes from GW's camera and then received an alert that a car had passed the first motion detectors.

"GW, get on back up here, someone's coming. It's probably the girls and Jeff, but we need to be prepared for the worst."

"I agree, let's hide in the woods behind the cabin until we know who is approaching."

They went about a hundred feet into the woods and found a place with a couple of dead trees to hide behind that afforded a good view of the area around the sheds and remains of the cabin.

Mary looked up in the mirror and saw the flashing blue lights, slowed down and pulled over to the side of the road.

"I was speeding and that cop has to do his thing and give me a ticket and then we will head on to the cabin."

The county sheriff's car sat behind them for 10 minutes and then the cop got out and approached the car as if it was full of terrorists.

Mary had her window down and her hands on the steering wheel as the cop approached her.

"Mam, are you in a big hurry? You were doing seven miles per hour over the speed limit. Now we want you and your family to get home safe today so I need your license and I'm going to write you a reminder to drive a bit slower."

Mary handed him her license and said, "Yes sir."

He walked back to his cruiser and sat there writing the ticket for over ten minutes. Mary looked back and he was eating donuts and drinking coffee for most of the time. He finally got out of the cruiser and slowly walked back to the van.

"Mam, please sign right there and you can get back on your way. Now drive safe and obey the speed limit."

"Yes sir."

Mary gave a left turn signal and pulled back on the road making sure that she was below the speed limit until the cop was out of sight.

"I'm glad that we covered the shotguns. We are about thirty minutes away from the cabin according to Grumpy's directions and the GPS."

"Hold your locations! That van that is supposed to be sitting back near the lodge on your tracking device just drove past us. And is 15 minutes from you."

"Damn, are you sure?"

"Yes, I could see their faces and it's definitely them. I'll bet you're glad I suggested keeping a look out back on the main road."

"Don't pat yourself too much until this is over. Men hide and hold your positions. Keep the main targets in sight while we wait for an opportunity."

"GW, the motion detector just went off again for the first ones by the main road. I don't like this. Keep your eyes peeled."

GW searched the area for intruders, found nothing for 15 to 20 minutes and then said, "It's our group. They're over there and coming straight at us."

He didn't see the men that had been watching them for 30 minutes.

GW and Grumpy came out of hiding and welcomed their families and Jeff.

"Mary did y'all go past the first detector twice?"

"No we drove straight here."

"Did you see anyone or tracks of anyone after leaving the main road?"

"No, but a hunter could have crossed in front of it with a four wheeler."

"It's not hunting season."

"Okay, a poacher or just people our running their four wheelers."

"Just the same let's all keep a look out for intruders. Jeff, take the shotgun and patrol around this area and watch for any movement while GW and I explore the sheds. We have found two decayed bodies so far, but that only makes the case stronger against Jack Jr. We need evidence that links his father and maybe his grandfather to the crimes."

GW added, "Work in pairs and keep an eye out for anything suspicious. Martha and Kathy take the area behind the cabin on the left; Mary and Sam take the area behind the cabin and to the right. We want to be back at the Lodge before dark so we only have about five hours to search today. I plan to do the same thing tomorrow. Let's get after it."

GW opened the shed door and the smell overwhelmed them. Sammy walked into the shed just as GW opened the trap door and sneezed and ran out of the shed. He jumped in Sam's arms and trembled.

Sam held little Sammy and said, "I've never saw him afraid of anything. He usually is fearless. The smell of death must scare him."

Sammy begged to get in the van and lay down in the floor for hours while the others searched. Sam tried to get him to go with her, but he wouldn't get out of the van.

Sam and Mary walked out in the woods and quickly noted the little red flags left by the police investigators. They kept walking past them until they were about 75 yards behind the cabin. Sam went back and stole the flags to mark their search. They staked out an area 25 yards wide by 50 yards long and walked over every square inch and found nothing until Sam was walking along and stumbled because of a depression in the soil. Mary came and helped her to her feet and they found several more depressions. The weeds and undergrowth kept them hidden.

"Sam, these are about the size you would need to bury a person. You literally stumbled on a graveyard. Let's keep looking before we tell Grumpy."

They staked out another area and found that the graves kept going at least another fifty yards further.

"Hey Grumpy, come back here and bring GW."

Grumpy had wondered how long it would take everyone to start calling him Grumpy, but he was getting used to the name. He got GW's attention and they walked back to the woods.

"Look here right in front of you at this low spot. There are 50 to a hundred low spots like this covering the entire area starting about 75 yards behind the cabin."

Grumpy went back to the van, grabbed an entrenching shovel and dug into the low spot. He only dug a foot and a half when he found a skeleton.

He brushed the dirt away from the skull and said, "Pay dirt. Look at the remaining clothes and shoes. This body has been here for 40-50 years. We have the father and grandfather."

GW went back to the shed while Grumpy dug up five other graves to find more skeletons.

"Dad, shouldn't we call the cops now and let them take over the case?"

"Not yet, and I plan to call the FBI tomorrow and get them involved. I saw an IU pin on one of the girls dress and think that might be enough to convince them that this is a federal case since one of the girls may have been abducted from Indiana."

Grumpy looked at his watch and said, "Girls and Jeff, I want y'all to leave now and GW and I will follow about 15 minutes behind you. I want you to come back to the Lodge from the west and we'll arrive from the east. See you back there."

"Dad, can Jeff and I ride back with you in the Jag. We never have ridden in such a nice car."

"Okay, just wait for us to leave."

They rest loaded up and left to head back to the Lodge. Sammy stayed in the van with Kathy.

"Grumpy, come down here I want to show you something."

Grumpy wet a handkerchief, placed it over his nose and mouth and stepped down into the hidden chamber. He saw GW shinning his flashlight on a section of the wall the furthest away from the cabin.

GW pulled at something and he was now pulling on a ring attached to the wall. Slowly a section of the wall moved. The wall had an axel in the middle and pivoted on it to open.

"Look a hidden chamber in the hidden chamber. Come on in with me."

Grumpy walked in and saw a tunnel going as far as the eye could see.

"The light shines at least 50 feet down that tunnel. We can't explore it today, but I want to check it out before we call the FBI.

"GW, I agree, this snake has bought his way out of every dastardly crime so far. I want to bury him."

They closed the pivoting door and went back up into the shed, left and closed the door. Jeff and Sam were sitting in the back seat of the car holding hands. On the drive back they discussed the day so far not noticing they were being followed a mile back thanks to the tracking device.

"Deke, we are following the main targets back to the Lodge. The girl is with them. We overheard they are going back to the cabin early tomorrow. Deke, they found a couple of

173

bodies under a shed and we think they found more graves a hundred yards or so behind the cabin. We will stay with them and report to you if anything changes. Awaiting your instructions."

"Take a quick look at the bodies in the shed and the graves out back and report back to me ASAP."

"Will do."

Deke reflected on the information, left his office and joined his wife and three children in the living room.

"Hon, I like having you home with the girls. I know that you start your new job Monday, but the girls really like having their daddy home with them."

He rolled on the floor playing with his girls and thinking that he was glad that Collins didn't want him to kill that teenage girl.

"Deke, those are all bodies of young girls. The two in the shed have only been dead for a week or less; the others span many years. Who the hell owns this cabin and what kind of monster is he?"

"Let me worry about that end of the business. The bad guys are the ones you are tracking and need eliminating. Tell the boys I am doubling their pay for this assignment. That will help you bear the stench for a couple more days."

"Thanks boss, but that isn't necessary."

"Yes it is; spend it wisely."

Deke thought out what he was going to say and called Jerry at the hotel, "Jerry, I'd like to meet with you this evening. I'll come to the hotel."

"I'll meet you in the bar at 8:00."

"Mr. Collins, this is Deke."

"Yes Deke. How bad was the accident?"

"No accident today. The girl was in the way. I need to fill you in on some issues that popped up today."

Collins was getting mad and blurted, "Are you saying that you can't handle the issues?"

"No sir, I believe that the targets found some left over issues from your son. There are two decaying bodies in a shed and a lot of graves about a hundred yards behind the cabin."

"Damn, they just had to go poking around. Is there a way to eliminate the shed and its bodies at the same time the targets have an accident?"

"Deke thought for a minute, "I believe that the cabin was blown up killing your son. He might have left some booby traps that could be stumbled upon."

"Do it even if it takes out every one of the snooping bastards."

"Yes sir."

Deke called his team leader and told him to place enough explosives in the shed to destroy the bodies and all of the targets when they return.

"Boss, do you mean to kill the children also?"

"Yes, and they are not children. Our customer wants to leave no loose ends."

"Yes sir. Kill them all."

Deke saw Jerry sitting at the bar flirting with the rather attractive bartender.

"Jerry, I see you are busy. Should I come back later?"

Jerry laughed and said, "Let's get a booth over in the corner. Joan, bring me rum and coke and a Black Jack and coke for my friend."

They seated themselves and waited on their drinks.

"So the team didn't get a chance to pull the trigger today."

"No the girl was in the wrong place several times. Deke, there may be a hundred bodies of young girls buried behind that cabin. What businesses does Collins run on the side?"

"Not my business or your for that matter. He has a different security group protecting those endeavors. I wouldn't ask about that either. I don't want to get a phone call about you one day."

Jerry laughed and ordered another round of drinks while Deke shared his plan to solve the target and bodies issues.

Deke drove home and went over the day's events in his head and thought, *"I need to develop a retirement plan."*

They all got back to the lodge and bathed to get the dirt and stench off them from the decaying bodies. They met in the lobby at 7:00, went into the dining room and asked for a private room to dine in. There were a couple of empty rooms so it wasn't a problem.

Grumpy got their attention and started saying grace, "Lord thank you for keeping us out of harm's way today, thank you for helping us search for the truth and to seek justice for these wrong doers. Finally thanks for this food and all of the blessings that you have bestowed on us. Amen."

"Grumpy, after supper I'm heading out to a store to get some kind of mask or gasmask to wear while we are in the shed. That smell took away my appetite and I had to scrub myself and throw my clothes away to get rid of the smell."

"Get me a mask also and you might buy some cheap sweat pants and T-shirts for us to work in and throw away tomorrow."

"Good idea, I'll also get a couple of stronger flashlights."

*

Chapter 14

They repeated the same scenario the next morning and arrived safely at the cabin. There was no need for tracking devices since they knew the targets were going back to the cabin. The only difference was that the assassination team never left the woods around the cabin. Jerry and Deke had joined them during the night and wanted to make sure no one fumbled this time.

"Grumpy, here is your mask and I guess it's time to go back down in the tunnel. Same as yesterday. Jeff will be on guard duty while the girls map out the rest of the graves."

Sammy was acting better today, but still not quite himself yet. He stayed close to Sam as they walked over the ground behind the cabin looking for more graves. Martha and Kathy searched the left side of the ever-widening graveyard and Mary and Sam the right side. They placed little marker flags for every depression.

"GW, this tunnel is lined with old clay bricks and has an old kerosene lantern hanging every 100 feet or so. I'll bet this tunnel dates back to before the civil war. It might be part of the underground railway to free slaves. Quite a few of the bricks have fallen and the tunnel could collapse at any time. "

"I just wish those girls had used it to escape from those monsters. I can't help but think God knew about this massacre and did nothing about it. It makes me sick."

"God gave mankind free will and by doing so we are able to do good and bad. God doesn't step in and save every person from the bad guys. He has good guys like you and me to try to stop the bad guys."

"I wish we had looked for a satellite map of this area. This tunnel has to lead to another building or house. Watch out more bricks on the floor!"

GW and Grumpy had walked down the tunnel about 100 yards when they came to a door with a heavy lock. They pried on it with a screwdriver, but only managed to break the screwdriver.

"Let's go to the van and get a tire tool to twist the lock off. We can check on the girls and see how they are doing. We probably need to tell them about the tunnel."

Jeff was sitting on a fallen tree scanning the area towards the front of the cabin when he heard, "Drop the shotgun sonny."

He quickly turned to see his attackers and was struck on the head for his effort. He fell to the ground dazed.

"Damn Joe, "You knocked him out. I don't want to have to carry him back to the shed."

They gagged him, tied his feet and hands and waited for instruction.

Martha and Kathy were not finding as many graves and hoped they were almost done searching. Kathy heard a grunt and looked up just as Martha was drug behind a tree. Before she could yell, a hand covered her mouth and she heard, "If you want to live keep your mouth shut."

Without thinking, she lashed out at the attackers and hammered an elbow into the man trying to grab her from behind. He doubled over and released her. She whirled around and caught the other man by surprise and her right foot hit him in the groin. He vomited as he fell to the ground. She didn't see the third man as he clubbed the back of her head with his pistol.

The third man tied a gag over her mouth and her hands behind her back. Another pushed her Nana towards her and then tied and gagged her.

The man, who had been kicked, slowly got up and pulled his pistol, placed it against the unconscious girls head and said, "I'll end this bitch's life right now."

"And we'll have to kill you if you do. You're just mad because she whipped your ass."

"That was a sucker punch. Who would have guessed the girl was a Ninja?"

"Well three down and four to go. Watch these while I help the others get the last two women. Then we can sit back and watch them all go boom."

Sam looked up to see a man grabbing Mary just as Sammy started growling behind her. She turned to see Sammy biting a man on the hand and growling like a wolf. She reached in her fanny pack, sprayed the man's face with Mace and kicked him in the shin. Sammy ran to help Mary and started attacking the man who held her. The man kicked Sammy and almost killed him. Sammy charged again, but the man was very fast and kicked Sammy again. Sammy lay on the ground whimpering. Sam saw this and ran over to him, but was grabbed from behind by two men and quickly tied and gagged. Sammy looked at her and then his head dropped and his eyes closed.

The men were taking their captives to the shed just after GW and Grumpy got back to the shed with the tire tool.

A man yelled from behind them, "Drop your guns and turn around slowly. I will shoot the women so don't do anything funny."

GW and Grumpy dropped their guns and held their hands in the air. They saw several men bring the girls towards the shed and another two were carrying Jeff. They lined them all up in front of the shed and one of the thugs pulled out his phone and took pictures of them.

181

Two men walked up and one said, "So these are the people causing your boss so much trouble. It's too bad that you won't live much longer, but the boss warned you several times and you wouldn't listen. Take them in the shed and untie them. We can't have them found with their hands and mouths all tied up, can we. Before you close the door, throw their weapons in with them. Don't get any ideas about shooting at us; we will shoot back."

He held up a device that looked like a walkie-talkie and said, "Your cell phones won't work, thanks to this little blocking device."

Kathy stepped forward and said, "Are you the men that killed my mom and dad; the Coles?"

She turned and faced Jerry and tried to kick him, but only managed to fall down.

Jerry responded, "Shut up and die like your parents did in that mine shaft."

One of the men picked her up and threw her into the shed.

They carried Jeff into the shed and then forced the others into the shed. At the last minute, they threw the two pistols through the closing door.

"Now you need to say your prayers while we clean up around the area. You are about to meet your God when we blow this shed to little tiny pieces."

"Mary said, "What died in here, the smell is horrible."

Grumpy said, "Everyone stay on this end of the room, there are two decaying bodies over there."

"GW, one of the guys also mentioned watching us go boom. I think they planted explosives in the shed."

Grumpy said, "GW let's go downstairs and get as far down that tunnel as we can."

Grumpy opened the hatch and GW and the girls scrambled down the steps. GW opened the hidden door and started pushing his loved ones and friends through the door. He gave Martha a flashlight and told her and the others to run as far down the tunnel as they could. Grumpy lowered Jeff down to GW, then felt around the floor of the shed for the pistols, and found both. He took one last look and jumped down to the floor below. They picked Jeff up and they moved as fast as they could down the tunnel and away from the shed. GW kicked the door closed as he got through the doorway.

Just as they caught up to the others the ground shook and the roof fell in in front of them. Pelted with bricks dirt and debris, the shockwave pounded them. The noise was thunderous and a cloud of dust choked their lungs. A brick struck Grumpy above his right ear and he fell with Jeff to the ground. GW had also been knocked to the ground, but quickly recovered. He shook Grumpy, who tried to get up, but fell back down.

"GW, check on the others while I get my head straight. I'm seeing stars and bright lights."

GW found his flashlight and aimed it ahead to see several legs sticking out of the debris ahead. He started moving bricks and dirt away from the women. Mary shoved the bricks off her and started digging also. She found Kathy and drug her out of the rubble and started digging again. By this time, Grumpy had joined them and they freed Sam and Martha at last.

Martha said, "Is everyone ok? Check yourself out for any broken bones and sharp pains."

Sam replied, "Mary covered me and my baby so I'm ok except for a knot on the back of my head."

Kathy replied, "Same here. My ankle feel's twisted and I have a bunch of bruises from bricks falling, but I'll be okay."

Everyone had the same story of bruises, bumps and sprains. Jeff, still unconscious, appeared to be uninjured.

"That blast levelled the place around the shed and probably blew the van and Jag to bits. We are trapped and will have to dig our way out."

"Yeah, Grumpy, we have three choices. Go up through the roof or dig out the tunnel ahead or behind us."

Grumpy shinned his flashlight at the ceiling and said, "GW, we are about twenty feet underground and I don't want to get buried. Let's dig away from the shed."

"I agree. Let's get started.

GW and Grumpy started moving bricks off the pile from the top and the girls pitched them back behind them.

"I only plan to make a small hole for us to climb over this pile of bricks."

The bricks were easy to move, but there was a lot of dirt mixed in from the cave in. They had to shove the dirt behind them with their hands, which were now bloody from scrapes and cuts.

"GW, I think it's open in front of me. Shine the light over here."

GW shined the light in front of Grumpy and there was a small hole. They feverishly grabbed bricks and passed them back to the women to dispose of.

"I think that I can get through."

Grumpy wiggled his way through, pointed the flashlight down the tunnel and said, "We're through. I can see the locked door."

Grumpy worked from the other side while they enlarged the opening. He had them place dirt on the bricks so they could slide Jeff through the opening.

"I don't want anyone to come through yet. I'm going to use my .45 to blast the lock off the door. The bullet will ricochet and you might get killed."

They agreed and Grumpy aimed at the lock so that the bullet wouldn't glance back on him and pulled the trigger. The bullet hit the lock and ricocheted bouncing off the walls, but missed Grumpy.

"Stay there, it didn't break the lock. It always works in the movies. Cover your ears again."

He fired a round and the lock careened to the side of the tunnel."

Grumpy asked Mary to come through the small opening so they could pull Jeff through to the other side. They got Jeff through and then all of the others wormed their way through.

Sam made it through and said, "Somewhere in all of those maternity books is a paragraph that says, "Don't get shot at, don't climb over a pile of bricks and especially don't get blown up. It could cause harm to the baby."

They all choked down their laughter, because they knew how true that was.

The door still wouldn't open until GW remembered that he had the blade of the broken screwdriver in his pocket. He wedged it between the sill and the door and pried the door open to reveal more of the same type tunnel. They travelled for several minutes and another door blocked their escape. This door was unlocked. Grumpy opened it to reveal a large dark room. They could see large boxes and machinery.

Grumpy thought for a minute and said, "Turn off the flashlights."

It took several seconds for their eyes to adjust, but they saw several places where light was streaming in to the room. Grumpy turned his flashlight on and walked around the room examining the walls. He tripped a couple of times because the room had a lot of old machinery stacked randomly around on the floor.

"This is a basement to an old warehouse or factory."

Grumpy found an opening in one wall that led to a set of stairs. He walked up the steps and opened the door to see a dimly lit room. He yelled for the others to join him. They found a place to lay Jeff down and started to explore the building.

In a few minutes, Jeff came to and said, "I wanted to drive the Jag. Where am I? Where is Sam? Is she safe? My head hurts."

Sam was by his side holding his hand. She bent over and gave him a peck on the forehead.

"I knew that head was too hard to dent. Welcome back to the world of spies, detectives and people trying to kill us.

Grumpy interrupted with, "Well Collins will soon be told that his worries are over. He will think that we are all dead. GW we need a plan. The police will arrive any minute and in a couple of days the headlines will read that some bungling want to be detectives tripped a booby trap set by Collins Jr. and Sr. will be off the hook."

"The creeps didn't take our cell phones. I'll call a friend in the FBI who owes me a favor. I'll get him to get the FBI involved."

Sam said, "Please hold that call GW, I think that we should have a plan before Collins figures out that we are alive and tries to kill us again. If that shed had not been connected to the tunnel, we would all be dead. My baby and I want to live just a little longer."

"You are right, sorry, I had my cop hat on and need to place my Gramps hat on and think about all of your safety."

Jeff raised his head and said, "Where is the fur ball?"

Sam started crying and said, "Those men hurt him. They kicked him until he had to stop trying to save me. He ran off into the woods and is probably dead."

Mary held her while she cried.

Grumpy said, "You may be right, but that is one tough ball of fur. Let's pray for him. Heavenly father, you sent Sammy down to earth to be Sam's guardian angel and he has saved several of us over the past few months. Please look over him and protect him. If he has passed, please take him in your arms and find a place in heaven for this brave little dog. Amen."

*

Chapter 15

Deke reported the events to Collins that afternoon. Sweeping their presence from the area, he stayed at the site and instructed his team to remove all of the marker flags. There was nothing left except for the crater where the shed had been and two burned out hulks of the van and the Jaguar. Blown down trees were in a circle of 100 yards around the blast site. Several small fires had started, but burned out before the police arrived. He assigned several of his team to monitor the police radio chatter and he personally told his snitch to call him with any info, as it was available from the KSP.

"Mr. Collins, we had to eliminate all of the targets. There were no survivors and there is a blast crater about 50 feet across where that shed had been. We removed any trace of our presence and moved back to local hotels where we can monitor the police. I will keep you posted."

"Pardon me, but I have heard that Bill Jones was taken care of before and he keeps popping back up."

"Mr. Collins, we put him in a hole under that shed that was packed with C4, closed the door and blew it to tiny bits. If he comes back to haunt you, it will be as an angel."

Collins laughed and got off the phone.

Deke received a report from his team on his way home and told the team leader to send all but himself and a person to monitor the police channels home. The job done, he just wanted to be able to react if a surprise came up.

"Give the team my thanks and tell them the money is being deposited in their accounts in the morning."

He arrived at his home and his wife had the news on TV. The announcer was talking about the blast over in eastern Kentucky. He said that early reports said that no one could have survived the tremendous blast and that investigators were sifting through the wreckage of two vehicles to determine who the owners were. The announcer noted that the blast was at the crime scene where Jack Collins Jr. blew himself up along with the family cabin. The announcer speculated that someone trespassing might have set off a hidden booby trap set there by Collins Jr.

"Darling, isn't that the family that owns the company that you are going to work for?

"I don't know. They have the same last name."

By noon on Monday, they were showing the pictures and names of the Cole and Jones' families as missing and potentially killed in the blast. A few hours later Jeff Stone's name was added to the list of missing and potentially dead.

"Deke, did you hear the news. That blast probably killed seven people. There were three kids killed and one was a 15-year-old pregnant girl. What kind of sick person kills 15-year-old children? Also, your boss's cabin was used by his son to rape, torture and kill little girls. Are you sure that your boss is not involved?"

"Darling, his son was one sick dude, but Mr. Collins is a good man and will soon be the governor of Kentucky. You don't get elected to be the governor if you are a pedophile."

"I guess you are right. I just wanted to talk with someone because this story made me sick."

"I love you and you need to stop watching the news."

"Okay, see you at dinner."

He started thinking about his boss and that some of the bodies found at the cabin were there before Jack Jr. was born.

*

Chapter 16

They brain stormed for several hours and found that there was no foolproof plan that would put Collins in jail and stop attempts on their lives.

GW said, "We still don't have proof that Collins is involved and without that he will be a threat to us the rest of our lives."

Kathy pulled out her phone, started looking at pictures and a video and then said, "We may not have proof that Collins is involved, but can the police tie these men back to Collins? Look at these."

The pictures showed the faces of six of the ten men involved and had one of the two leaders telling their men to throw them in the shed and mentioning the explosion.

"Kathy, how did you get the pictures?"

I had my camera set for voice activation in my bra so I would have my hands free while working with Grandma. I just kept taking pictures every chance I got. They didn't search us because that wanted us to have our normal possessions when we died."

Jeff said, "Let me see that phone, please. I'm sending the pictures to my e-mail account and making sure, that they are backed up on Kathy's cloud. We can't lose them."

GW pulled a business card from his wallet and said, "Jeff please send them to this e-mail address and tell the agent that I will call him later today. Let's figure out how to get home."

Grumpy added, "Jeff, I'm going to call your mom and dad and tell him that you are alive, but they can't tell anyone then I'll hand you the phone."

They went outside of the old building and had a decent cell signal. Jeff's parents had just talked with the police and told them that Jeff had gone on vacation with the Jones. It hadn't sunk in he might be dead, so they had been spared pain by the call. Grumpy briefly explained the need to keep the fact they know Jeff and the Jones were alive to themselves. Jeff spoke to his parents and quickly got off the phone.

"Thank God we called when we did; it was just dawning on them that I might be dead. Dad is renting a large passenger van and coming to pick us up. I told him that we would call him in an hour and let him know where to pick us up."

"We should be able to find the main road if we just walk north a few miles. Heck this factory may be on the main road. We may not have to walk very far at all."

GW and Kathy walked to the end of the driveway and came back a half hour later.

GW said, "Tell your dad to turn right at the first drive past mile marker 6 on Highway 119 and go down that road until he sees the old factory. We will wait here for him."

Jeff made the call and his mom and dad arrived about three hours later.

Grumpy walked up to Jeff's parents and said, "Hello, Adam and Ellen. I want to say how sorry that I am that we put you through this scare."

Jeff's mom replied, "Have you called the police? We passed a road two miles back that the police had blocked off and there were ambulances and fire trucks leaving as we passed."

GW spoke up and said, "I have contacted the FBI. We are afraid that some of the KSP and Local police have been bought off by the ones responsible for the attempt on our lives."

"The news said that was a biker gang that attacked you last week. Was that true?"

Grumpy replied, "We think that someone paid them to attack us to get us to stop investigating Jack Collins Jr."

"Is my son safe now or will they come back and try to kill us all."

"We are all safe because they think that we are all dead. They won't bother you, but we need them to think that we are dead for a while to give the FBI a chance to catch them. We have proof against the ones who attacked us today and there is enough proof back at the cabin to put Collins Sr. away when the FBI investigates the explosion."

"Thanks for filling us in. Y'all must be starving so let's stop at the next restaurant and grab some burgers."

Mary replied, "Great, we haven't had anything to eat since 5:00 this morning."

They stopped at a fast food restaurant and had burgers and fries in the van. They were filthy and smelled of dead bodies.

"Grumpy, I'm going to call my FBI friend and give him the story."

"Ok, we'll finish eating and leave when you are finished."

While they were finishing their supper, Sam whispered to Grumpy, "Dad, we have to go back and find Sammy."

"Sam, I'm so sorry that I forgot about our little buddy. We can't go back there, but I know who can."

Grumpy called the PI that he had working on the Collin's case.

"Hello, this is Bill. I have a job for you that I need completed tomorrow. There is an extra $500 over your normal fee."

"Bill, I'll be glad to help you. What do you need?"

Grumpy explained the situation and the PI agreed to find Sammy and keep the detail to himself. He told Grumpy that this must be a special dog because his bill would be about two grand for the search.

"Bill I'll need something that Sam wore to help me get close to the dog. I'll be right by in a couple of hours to pick the article up."

GW made the call and his friend answered the phone on the first ring.

"GW, I received that message and pictures. It sounded like you are lucky to be alive. I checked my sources and they indicated that the explosion wiped out half the trees for a hundred yards around that cabin. How did you escape the men and get away?"

GW told him about the tunnel and how they used it to get away from the blast. He went on to explain the pictures and video to the agent. He then backed up and filled his friend in on the situation with his son's disappearance and Collin's involvement.

"GW, of course I won't be on the case, but I have turned the information over to the Kentucky office and they have a team heading to the blast site. The ATF will also get involved due to the explosions. I called them as soon as I saw the pictures and video. Keep me posted and stay safe my friend."

Mary called their family doctor and asked him to meet them at their house. He said that he had heard the news and had assumed that they were dead. He understood the need for secrecy and said that he would check Sam and Jeff out as soon as they got home.

They arrived home later that evening to see Dr. Rogers sitting in his car. They all went into the house and he checked Jeff out first.

195

"Well, you don't have any signs of concussion, take aspirin for the headache and I'll drop by your house after work tomorrow to check on you. Didn't you get a concussion last week?"

"No I had a bump on my head, but thank God that I have a hard head."

"Jeff we will have to get you examined at the hospital as soon as you can go without being in danger. Sam, getting blown up is not good for a baby."

"I promise that I'll try to avoid bombs and tunnel collapses in the future."

"The baby's heartbeat is strong and you didn't get hit in the stomach so it looks good. I need you in my office tomorrow so I can perform an ultra sound to make sure that the baby is ok."

He checked everyone out and Grumpy walked him to the door.

"Doc, bill me for Jeff's charges. I don't think his parents should be on the hook for my problems."

"Bill, I'll bill everything to insurance and the rest is my donation to putting that SOB Collins in jail. No one has had the courage to stand up to him. If you don't stop him he will become Governor."

"Doc, I see why people backed down. He never stops coming at you. I'm willing to go toe to toe with him, but he almost killed Sam and Mary."

"Well, God is with you and I'll pray for you regardless. Get some sleep and be careful."

Jeff went home with his parents after giving Sam a hug and kiss on her cheek.

196

Mary said, "I'm having some ice cream while you two brains figure out the next move."

Sam, Kathy and Martha joined them in the kitchen and they all had a big bowl of butter pecan ice cream. Sam was moping around because she missed Sammy. The women joined GW and Grumpy in the living room and they discussed their plans for the upcoming week.

GW took the lead, "We have to stay here out of sight until the FBI arrests Collins and his henchmen. We can't let anyone see us or we will be in danger all over again."

"Let's turn on the TV and see what the news has to say about us and the explosion. It's 10 minutes until the 10:00 news starts."

Sam turned the TV on and changed the channel to their favorite channel for news. The lead story was about a drug dealer killed in Lexington; an overhead picture of the area around the cabin appeared on the TV. The announcer told about the huge blast and that seven local people were missing and feared dead from the blast. The news showed the burned out hulks of the van and jag next to a large hole in the ground. The scene reminded Mary of a volcanic eruption that she had seen on TV when Mount Helens blew up.

When the story ended Martha exclaimed, "All of our friends and loved ones will think that we are dead. Tomorrow we will see Grumpy's friends saying what a good guy he was and it is a shame his life ended so tragically. Then we'll hear that GW and Grumpy were "want to be" detectives who stumbled on a left over booby trap from Collins Jr. and they should have left the investigation to the pros."

Sam replied, "No, we will hear that nothing significant happened in the world yesterday because Jack Collins Sr. said so and vote for Collins for Governor."

"Sam that was the best sarcastic comment I have ever heard. Very funny."

The next morning GW's cell phone was ringing and it took him a minute to clear his head to answer it, "This is GW."

"Mr. Cole. I'm agent Anderson with the FBI. A friend of ours showed me the pictures and told me your story. There are twenty news reporters outside Mr. Jones home right now. My team is unloading their gear in the driveway and will be entering the house in 10 minutes. Get dressed and ready to tell us about your adventure. We want the bad guys to think they were successful so stay away from windows."

"Okay, we will be ready in 10 minutes."

GW and Martha woke up the rest and they were dressed and ready for the onslaught of FBI and ATF Agents.

The front door opened and Agent Anderson walked in with three other agents and said, "Those two work for me and this lady is ATF Agent Winters. She is interested in the explosives in the shed.

Grumpy looked at Agent Winters and said, "You questioned us after the explosion that leveled the cabin. That was dynamite at the cabin; this was C4 at the shed. I only had a second, but there were 20-30 blocks of it in the hole under the shed all wired into a tool bag."

The Agents set up three rooms to question each of them separately. They also searched the entire house, garage and grounds for evidence.

Mary saw several of her friends from church holding hands and crying.

She said, "Oh my God, what are we putting these poor people through. We have to stop this before they have a funeral for us."

After several hours, Anderson asked for Grumpy and GW to meet with them alone.

"We have been trying to shut down Collins Industries for five years. This case is the closest that we've come to finding his hands on a crime, but still no luck. We have caught the leader and two of his thugs at the airport. They all lawyered up and we won't get anything out of them. The rest have disappeared. These guys are all ex Special Forces gone bad and hire out to do wealthy peoples dirty work. The leader, Jerry, has been on our radar for 10 years and he kept slipping through our fingers. Even now, one of the best criminal lawyers in the country is flying into Louisville to represent him and the other two."

"What about Collins? We won't be safe as long as he is walking the streets."

"We have teams digging up bodies from all around that cabin. The local and State Police are pissed that we took over the investigation, but they bungled the first investigation. The bodies date back for over 50 years from the clothing and jewelry found in the graves, but we'll know more when the crime lab does its work. The problem is that there is no evidence linking Collins to the murders or the sex trafficking. We are meeting with him and his lawyers in the morning, but don't think it will go anywhere. He won't have a clue how the bodies got on his property. We are also opening a case on the friend of Kathy's. Bridgette Payne. It's too early to tell if this Ms. Tapp is involved with Collins.

"So we have to look over our shoulders for the rest of our lives?

"Yes, that would be prudent. I'm personally going to tell him in front of his lawyers that the FBI will be watching him very closely. We have found two of his managers in other cities who can be linked to a myriad of crimes. He doesn't want the publicity. Now the sticky part; I need you and GW to stop investigating him on your own. You have scared the crap out of him and he is handling it as a cleanup operation. You stop and let us handle it and I'll bet he stops."

Grumpy got red in the face and said, "So he tries to kill us and we stop the investigation and the bad guy wins."

"Grumpy, I'm not going to sugar coat this; you two and your families are lucky to be alive. Stop and you will probably be left alone; keep investigating and you will be dead. We can't stop him. We can't put you in witness protection because you are not testifying against him and he has an army of thugs working for him.

GW chimed in, "So the killers of my son and daughter will never be caught and I'm supposed to look the other way?"

"GW, the killers of your family are dead and probably at the bottom of a mineshaft somewhere here in Kentucky. Collin's last security chief went missing along with several of his staff and some of their associates. One survivor left the country and is hiding in South America. I'm certain they are responsible for the original attacks on the Jones family and your son and his wife. We are closing those cases."

"So no justice and we have to shut up!"

"Look, we don't like it any more than you do, but if you want your kids and wives to live long happy lives, stop stirring things up and leave the investigation to us. Now, we need to let everyone know that you are alive. By the way, Collins doesn't know that you are alive yet. I get to tell him and wipe that smug look off his face."

"So what do we tell everyone?"

"Just tell them the truth except don't mention the tunnel. Just say you escaped out the back door. I want to keep the tunnel secrete until we finish the investigation."

"Okay so we go on TV with you after your meeting with Collins and say that we escaped and went to the police."

"Yes, just stick to that. Oh, also just say that there were only five of them. We will ID the missing two and perhaps the others won't flee the country if they don't think that we are looking for them. Under no circumstance should you mention that the explosion took place on the Collins property. Don't say why you were there. Just tell any reporters that there is an ongoing investigation and you can give out any more info."

Deke was watching TV with his wife and girls when his phone rang.

"Is this Deke White? The head of Collins Security Group?"

"Yes, I'm Deke White. What can I do for you?"

"I have some very important information for you and Mr. Collins. I need $5,000 for this info and then I'll keep sending info as it develops. I have contacts in the FBI and you need to hear what I have to say."

"What does the information concern?

"Jerry and his companions"

"Okay, I'll pay you $5,000 for this and we'll see what else you can deliver."

"Jerry, Jim and Al were arrested by the FBI earlier today. It involves the explosion on Collins' property. The targets were not eliminated."

Deke choked and couldn't talk for a minute and then replied, "That is interesting, but why should I pay for info on some explosion on Collin's property that doesn't involve him?"

"Because you want to make sure that your boss knows everything that the FBI has on him and his crime empire and get information on the ongoing investigation."

"Okay, meet me at the south entrance to the South Gate Mall at 7:30 in the morning. I'll have cash."

Deke called his wife into his office and said, "Darling, start packing for a vacation. We are leaving tonight and we will never return!"

Deke, opened his safe, threw all of the cash and gold into two bags and loaded them into his Expedition along with most of his weapons and ammunition. He knew that Collins had other pros like Jerry on his payroll and knew that this was the time to retire and go off the grid. He had bought a place in Costa Rica for retirement and disappearing was his only option. He thought about taking Collins out before he left, but wanted to get his girls far away as fast as possible.

"Dad, that's BS. Collins gets off scot-free again and girls keep being kidnapped and sold. That explosion probably killed Sammy. That's not right and isn't fair......"

Sam went on for several minutes yelling at Grumpy. Mary came over and held her close and stroked her hair until she stopped yelling."

"Look, I feel the same way, but I have to think about Mary, you and the baby. Collins can kill us any time he wants. He was just trying to make the explosion look like an accident or he could have had that team kill us all while driving to church. We can't protect ourselves against a man with unlimited resources and an army of professional killers. Think about your baby's and your safety."

"I know that you are right, but that doesn't make me feel any better."

"I know darling. I know."

Collins and three lawyers were in a conference room at his home office when his secretary called to say that the two FBI Agents were in the lobby."

"Have you been able to find Mr. White?"

"No sir. He doesn't answer his cell phone and there is no answer at his home."

Collins looked across the table and said, "Phil, contact Jerry and have him on the phone after this meeting."

The door opened and Anderson walked in with the Director of the FBI for the Southern Region.

"Hello, I'm John Abernathy and this is Special Agent Anderson. Mr. Collins, do you think that you need three lawyers just to talk with us about a little old explosion on your property out in the sticks of Kentucky?"

"And you're from the government to help me."

"No Mr. Collins, we're from the government and we just want to find out why people in your employ keep breaking the law? We're wondering if we have a RICO case on our hands."

He handed Collins subpoenas for all Collins US Operations and said, "We have agents handing subpoenas to every manager of every operation that Collins Industries has in the USA. We are going to investigate every dime that you ever made or spent. We already have seen evidence of millions of dollars being sent to your off shore accounts from Saudi Arabia. We are also trying to figure out how Ms. Tapp fits in to your criminal activity."

Collins was calm on the outside, but turning red in the face and blowing up on the inside.

"Well I guess the only happy people in the room are these high priced lawyers. Oh, Agent Anderson has something to tell you."

"Mr. Collins, that explosion on your property has brought attention to the fact that there are over a hundred total bodies buried there. Every body found was a young girl. Oh and I almost forgot, Mr. Jones and Mr. Cole send you their best regards. They received a few scratches, but they and their families are forgetting you and going on with their lives. We have the people in custody that attacked the Jones and murdered the Coles. Yes, Jerry will be tough to crack, but one of his men will take a deal. WITSEC, relocation and a job to stay out of jail will sound good to one of these thugs. We have them nailed on attempted murder of the Cole and Jones

204

families. It's just time until one of them leads us to the person paying the bills."

Collins stayed calm and said, "I have nothing to do with anything you just said and Collins industries will be found innocent. You can talk with these men in the future. Now if you're done we'll show you the way out."

The Agents were ushered out of the room and Collins started yelling and throwing everything off the table. The FBI agents could hear the tirade and Anderson said, "I think that we upset his day."

That night Sam lay in bed crying and thinking about Sammy. She got out of bed, kneeled down and prayed.

"Dear God, please take care of my dog Sammy. He is just an innocent dog and hasn't done anything to hurt anyone that didn't deserve it. If he died in the explosion, please rub his belly and pat his head. He likes that. Amen."

Bridgette saw the news about the explosion killing the Jones, Coles and Jeff Stone. She was mad as hell and cried herself to sleep. Those were her friends. Then a couple of days later she saw Bill Jones and Kathy's Grandfather in the news saying that they escaped the explosion. They didn't mention Collins, but the info Jeff passed her indicated that Collins was the person buying at least half the girls. She knew what she had to do.

Sammy had been knocked unconscious by a kick from one of Collins men. The explosion woke him up to a foggy mind and he couldn't see or hear for most of the rest of the day. He found a hollowed out tree, climbed in and slept for two days. He woke up thirsty and hungry. He walked until he found a stream and drank while constantly on guard for those men who took his girl away. He sniffed the air and caught a slight whiff of her and her family. He walked cautiously in the direction the smell came from until he was back at the place where the shed had been. He saw many men walking around the area where the shed had been. Several had crawled down in the large hole. He didn't trust the men so he stayed out of sight. He got lucky and found a pile of garbage that had some French fries and half-eaten hamburgers and ate his fill. He slept behind a log for several hours and then started looking for Sam's smell. The air was thick with a strange burnt smell and he had to keep circling the blast site until he found her smell by a big building far away from where he'd last scene her. He followed her scent to the road and headed east until he lost her smell. He knew he was heading in the direction of home and thought he would find her there.

He got off the road, into the bushes and weeds when he saw a car. He knew that cars were dangerous even though he liked riding in them with his head out the window and his ears flapping. He missed his girl and knew that he had to be with her to protect her. He had walked over twenty miles when he saw the restaurant and snuck around to the backside of the building. A woman and a young girl who looked like his Sam were eating fried chicken on a picnic table behind the restaurant. Sammy starving, walked up to them and begged for food. He was so cute that they gave him some scraps and the woman poured water in a cup for him.

"Mom, he's such a cute dog. Can I keep him?"

"Hon, he has a tag on him and some other poor girl is probably looking for him right now."

The girl tried to catch Sammy and he bolted off into the woods.

The PI had scoured the area around the blast sight and even walked up to the police and showed them pictures of the missing dog. No one had seen Sammy. He had looked for two days and had only seen a few Beagles and mixed breeds loose in the area. He stopped at every store and gas station and posted a picture of Sammy with a $500 reward and his cell number. He drove up and down the roads and was about to give up when his phone rang.

"Are you the man offering the reward for the Shih Tzu?"

"Yes, have you seen him?"

"He was here at Bryan's Dairy Bar just twenty minutes ago. We tried to catch him, but he got away. He is heading down the road heading west. Don't forget the reward money."

"Okay."

He drove past the Dairy Bar slowly and kept looking for Sammy. He had to stop and let traffic go by so he could creep down the road. He stopped for the fifth time and caught a glimpse of a movement in the weeds.

"Sammy, come here. Sam wants to see you. I have her t-shirt."

He waived the shirt and Sammy ran up to the man and looked at him from about five feet away. He sniffed the man and got in the car with him. He laid his head on Sam's t-shirt and slept all of the way to the Jones home.

"Bill, I have Sammy. He's a little dirty and has a couple of cuts, but appears to be ok. I'll be at your home in about two hours."

"Thanks, I appreciate you doing this for me."

Grumpy got off the phone and called Sam into the kitchen where Mary was cooking. Jeff was with her and they both came in from the back yard.

"Ladies and Jeff, I have some good news. My PI found Sammy and they will be here in about two hours.

Sam hugged Grumpy and started crying.

*

Chapter 17

Bridgette woke up every morning at 6:00 am, exercised, read the local paper and viewed the national news on the internet. She had trained herself to keep her mind and body fit and sharp over the past several months. She ate fruit and granola for breakfast every morning and ate only healthy meals for lunch and supper. She had changed from a beautiful young girl into a beautiful young woman with an incredibly toned and fit body. She had bought a black Jeep Unlimited ragtop and a slightly used blue Explorer to replace the high mileage one that she bought in Lexington. She had all of the clothes and electronic gadgets that any young woman could possibly want. She was rich, sexy and bored to death. She didn't want a boyfriend yet and only yearned to get moving on her crime fighting career. She would still kill the drug pushers, but didn't need the money. She thought about charities and other ways to use the money to help people.

She had excelled in the self-defense and gun instruction courses and took advanced courses to hone the skills that she would need. She was already working on a black belt and was a better shot than the men were in her classes. She studied criminology in her spare time and was pleased to find case studies about crime. She delved into why criminals are caught. She also focused on drug related crimes and money laundering crimes. Her classes at KY Wesleyan were boring since she had to take mainly the prerequisites the first year. It cost a small fortune to get a transcript and other high school documents forged in a very short time, but she always found that cash talks loud and almost anyone could be bought.

Bridgette also took lessons to obtain her motor cycle license and rode one of her bikes every day. She purchased a three-year-old 500cc dirt bike and a customized old Harley soft tail. She bought the dirt bike because those skills might come in handy in her new profession.

She was ready for her first assignment. Jack Collins would never see it coming.

Mary left the kitchen to check on the baby while GW shuffled the cards for the next hand. Baby Jenn was a month old and becoming spoiled quickly. Grumpy and Mary watched little Jenn while Sam was in school and loved every minute of it. Grumpy had already bought more toys than the little girl could ever use. Jennifer Marie Jones was born a month after Sam's birthday and was 6 pounds 5 ounces. She had blonde hair and blue eyes. Sammy was very protective of her and couldn't wait to play with her.

Mary had Jenn in her arms when she heard the TV announcer interrupt the news for a special announcement concerning Jack Collins a potential candidate for Governor of Kentucky.

GW, Martha Bill, come in here now! There is a news flash about Collins and there are police cars in the scene in front of his business."

"Mary, have we missed anything?"

"No they are waiting on the KSP to make a statement. Look at the scrolling message at the bottom of the screen!"

It read, "**There has been a shooting at the main office of Collins Industries. One dead and three wounded**."

Several police officers walked up to the podium and the leader took the mic, "It is with deep regret that I have to announce that Jack Collins Sr. was shot and killed by a lone gunman this morning. The shooter shot Collins as he got out of his limo in the parking garage. The shooter also shot his three bodyguards and two are in critical condition at Baptist Hospital. The shooter appears to be a male about 5 feet 6 inches tall of medium build. He was wearing a black leather jacket and pants with black boots and a black helmet. He was riding a black dirt bike and headed east on highway 60. Witnesses described a black AK47 assault rifle and a black pistol of unknown caliber. We will update you as we gain information. We assure you that the shooter will be captured and prosecuted."

Grumpy quickly said, "While I know that this is a big relief for us, the proper thing to do is to pray for his soul."

Grumpy led the prayer, "God, we pray for his soul and hope that he repented for his sins before he died. Amen."

Sam and Jeff bumped fists and headed out to the back yard to sit at the picnic table and enjoy each other's company.

Grumpy heard Sam say, "I hope Mr. Collins burns in hell while all of those girls watch down from heaven."

Grumpy told the rest and they broke out laughing.

GW said, "Well I guess this adventure is over. Let's get back to playing cards."

Kathy watched Jeff and Sam leave and said, "I'm a little jealous, I was Sam's best friend, but now she has Jeff and baby Jenn."

"You are still her best girlfriend, godmother to Jenn and always will be. Boyfriends come and go best girlfriend crime fighters are forever."

"And I don't run and hide every time Sam breast feeds little Jenn."

"Kathy, that's normal for men to disappear when women have to take care of the kids."

Jeff made up an excuse, went straight home and got on his computer. He still had the account numbers and passwords for several of Jack Collins Sr.'s hidden bank accounts. He didn't want the money and would never steal a cent, but that money was earned by selling young girls in to slavery. He set up some dummy accounts in Switzerland and the Grand Caymans and moved over $300 million from Collins accounts to the new accounts. He would send money to each of the girls surviving parents or relatives and to anyone else harmed by Collins. The money was illegal and no accountant was tracking it. He left Collins Industries and Collins accounts in the USA intact. He wondered if anyone knew about the money besides a dead man and himself.

Over the next few weeks he hired a full time administrator, retained a lawyer and started a foundation to stop sex trafficking and another to help families search for missing children. He used a fake name and communicated solely through the phone and e-mail. The Administrators thought that the large endowments came from an overseas billionaire who was sending the money because his daughter had been kidnapped.

That night Mary caught Sam and said, "Darling, I think that you need to spend some quality time with Kathy. She's feeling a bit left out since the baby and Jeff take up so much of your time. Why don't you take her to the mall on Saturday and treat her to an afternoon at that new spa on me. Martha and I can go also, but we will stay out of your way."

"I like that; she has been acting strange lately. A trip to the mall is just what she needs.

THE END

Remember to post a good review if you like my novel.

Thanks AJ Newman

*

Books by AJ Newman

Alien Apocalypse:

The Virus   Surviving (Oct 2017)

A Family's Apocalypse Series:

Cities on Fire – Family Survival

After the Solar Flare - a Post-Apocalyptic series:

Alone in the Apocalypse   Adventures in the Apocalypse*

After the EMP series:

The Day America Died New Beginnings The Day America Died

Old Enemies The Day America Died Frozen Apocalypse

"The Adventures of John Harris" - a Post-Apocalyptic America series:

Surviving   Hell in the Homeland   Tyranny in the Homeland

Revenge in the Homeland...Apocalypse in the Homeland   John Returns

"A Samantha Jones Murder Mystery Thriller series:

Where the Girls Are Buried   Who Killed the Girls?

Books by AJ Newman and Cliff Deane

Terror in the USA: Virus: Strain of Islam

These books are available at Amazon:

http://www.amazon.com/-/e/B00HT84V6U

To contact the Author, please leave comments @:

www.facebook.com/newmananthonyj   Facebook page.

The Author

Anthony Newman has over 17 novels published on Amazon. He was born and raised in a small town in the western part of Kentucky. He and his best friend Mike spent summers shooting .22 rifles and fishing. He read every book he could get his hands on and fell in love with science fiction. He served six years in a National Guard Armored Unit and graduated from the University of Southern Indiana with a degree in Chemistry. He made a career working in manufacturing and logistics but always fancied himself as an author. He currently resides in Owensboro, Kentucky with his wife Patsy and a bunch of tiny mop dogs, Benny, Sammy, Cotton, and Callie.